"Tell Me The Truth, Shawnee,"

Ken said, his gaze caressing her face. "Weren't we in love back then? Or was I dreaming?"

She didn't want this. This was much too dangerous. "We barely knew each other," she said, using the same defense she'd used before and feeling less and less sure of it. "It felt like love, but..."

"If it wasn't love, you wouldn't have brought me up here that day," he said, his intense gaze daring her to contradict him.

He was right, and she knew it. Jade Tree Valley, her enchanted, magic world, her private place since childhood. She'd brought him here as a gift of love. And he'd given her a son in return.

"Maybe it *was* love," she whispered.

Dear Reader,

Welcome to March and to Silhouette Desire! Our *Man of the Month, Wrangler's Lady,* is from an author many of you have told me is one of your favorites: Jackie Merritt. But this story isn't *just* a *Man of the Month,* it's also the first book in Jackie's exciting new series, THE SAXON BROTHERS.

Next: HAWK'S WAY *is back!* Joan Johnston continues her popular series with *The Cowboy Takes a Wife,* where we learn all about Faron Whitelaw's— from *The Cowboy and the Princess*—half brother, Carter Prescott.

The tie-ins and sequels just keep on coming, with Raye Morgan's *The Daddy Due Date*—a tie-in to last month's *Yesterday's Outlaw*—and BJ James's *The Hand of an Angel,* which continues her terrific books about the McLachlan brothers.

If you're looking for something completely different, you *must* pick up *Carolina on My Mind* by Anne Marie Winston. Here, our hero and heroine are abducted by aliens . . . and that's just for starters! And if you're looking for *humor,* don't miss *Midnight Ice* by Cathie Linz.

Miniseries and tie-ins, bold men and adventurous heroines, the supernatural and humor . . . there's something for *everyone* here at Silhouette Desire. So enjoy.

All the best,

Lucia Macro
Senior Editor

Please address questions and book requests to:
Reader Service
U.S.: P.O. Box 1325, Buffalo, NY 14269
Canadian: P.O. Box 1050, Niagara Falls, Ont. L2E 7G7

RAYE MORGAN
THE DADDY DUE DATE

SILHOUETTE *Desire*®

Published by Silhouette Books

America's Publisher of Contemporary Romance

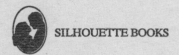 SILHOUETTE BOOKS

ISBN 0-373-05843-8

THE DADDY DUE DATE

Copyright © 1994 by Helen Conrad

This edition published by arrangement with Harlequin Enterprises B. V.

® and TM are trademarks of Harlequin Enterprises B. V., used under license. Trademarks indicated with ® are registered in the United States Patent and Trademark Office, the Canadian Trade Marks Office and in other countries.

Printed in U.S.A.

Books by Raye Morgan

Silhouette Desire

Embers of the Sun #52
Summer Wind #101
Crystal Blue Horizon #141
A Lucky Streak #393
Husband for Hire #434
Too Many Babies #543
Ladies' Man #562
In a Marrying Mood #623
Baby Aboard #673
Almost a Bride #717
The Bachelor #768
Caution: Charm at Work #807
Yesterday's Outlaw #836
The Daddy Due Date #843

Silhouette Romance

Roses Never Fade #427

RAYE MORGAN

favors settings in the West, which is where she has spent most of her life. She admits to a penchant for Western heroes, believing that whether he's a rugged outdoorsman or a smooth city sophisticate, he tends to have a streak of wildness that the romantic heroine can't resist taming. She's been married to one of those Western men for twenty years and is busy raising four more in her Southern California home.

In memory of Nick Howe, my son's best friend, who laughed at romance but was my French phrase expert anyway.

One

Ken Forrest parked the rented sedan in front of the little roadside store and looked up at the entrance. His heart was beating faster. That was pretty silly. There was nothing here but memories.

"You two settle down, now," Karen warned. Seated in the passenger seat, she half turned to keep an eye on the two youngsters in the back. "We'll be back at the hotel in a jiffy and you can go swimming in the pool. Okay?"

Ken didn't look at her, didn't notice her anxious glance at his face. She'd faded away and he was seeing this place as it had looked so long ago, when he'd arrived that morning, taking the steps two at a time, full of the need to see the beautiful girl again who worked behind the lunch counter. One look and he'd been filled with longing for her from the very beginning. One look and she'd entered his mind and his body in a way no other girl had ever done before or since.

So young. So long ago.

The windshield was dusty from the country roads they'd traveled on their sightseeing trip. He put up his hand as though to wipe away the dust, as though he could wipe away time, push back those years and find eighteen again.

"Are you going in?" Karen asked.

He looked at her, startled. He'd forgotten all about her and the kids.

"Yeah, I need..." Nothing. Nothing but to see that beautiful girl again. Nothing that was in any way possible. "I need a soda. You want anything?"

Karen shook her head. "No thanks. But maybe... how about some sugarless gum for the kids?"

He nodded absently, already forgetting as he stepped out of the car and slammed the door. He was going in. And his heart was beating faster, even though he knew she couldn't possibly be there. She was like a dream. She couldn't possibly ever be there again.

Shawnee never, ever came that way on a Friday, and when she did, she never ever stopped at Hiroshi's store. But today she'd been to Auntie Tam's and Auntie had talked forever and then forced her to take a barrelful of macadamia nuts, still in shells so hard you needed a small nuclear blast just to open them. She'd had to lug that barrel all the way down the hill to her car and she was hot and tired. She needed a cool drink before she finished the drive down the coast to her beachside home.

Besides, Hiroshi's had the best cracked seed plums and she thought she'd pick some up for Jimmy. The Hiroshis made it themselves from an old Chinese recipe instead of importing from Hong Kong like most stores did. She'd gorged on it when she'd worked here as a teenager, so many long years ago. It was the best on the island. So she headed for the driveway, parking off to the side because some tourist in a rented car had taken up the whole front parking area.

And when she looked up, her hand on the ignition key, she saw him.

He was going up the steps to the entrance, taking them two at a time, just like he always had. He was dressed differently—slacks and an open shirt instead of the jeans and jersey of the old days. And his golden hair was shorter, neater. But he was still long and lean and beautiful. Her heart stood still.

He disappeared into the store and she sat, not breathing, not thinking. And then she went into action, putting the car into reverse, backing out onto the highway again. It was a good thing no one was coming because she never looked. Her thoughts were a blur. She only knew she had to get out of there, drive like hell for home, and never look back.

Ken Forrest. She'd thought she would never see him again. There was a time when she would have given anything just to see him once more. But that feeling had died long, long ago. Now, all he did was scare her.

Arriving home, she drove the car around back, just in case, and ran into the house, dropping her clothes as she went, reaching into the bathroom for her swimsuit, tugging it on. Her long, chestnut hair was already in a thick braid down her back. It bounced against her tailbone as she ran toward the water's edge. In no time at all she was in the warm ocean water, swimming as hard as she could toward the little island that lay just inside the reef, working to block out the memories.

It didn't work. It never did. The memories were there, a part of her. If she didn't let them surface in the day, they wound their way into her dreams at night—and that was worse.

Why, oh, why, had he come back? She let herself see him again as he'd looked, going up the stairs. He was as long and lean as ever, his muscles just as hard as they had been when he'd held her all those years ago.

Eighteen years. A man was supposed to change in that amount of time. Suddenly she was angry with him. How dare he look even better now?

Where's your paunch, mister? she thought bitterly, biting her lip, hitting the water so that a spray leapt up, sparkling, toward the sky. Where are those sags and bags you're supposed to have?

Having reached the little island, she restlessly turned right around and kept swimming, her body cutting through the water, changing turquoise blue to silver, her mind back in that jungle valley on a warm summer afternoon. They had both been so young. Why did the young always have to pay such a steep price for their inexperience?

"Why now, Ken?" she moaned aloud, increasing her pace. "Why come back now?"

What had he been doing at the old store? Looking for her? There was no one left who would remember her there—and she had no idea who was living in her old house. They wouldn't be able to give him directions, either. She should be safe. Shouldn't she? There was no way he could find her.

"No way," she said aloud, talking to the sky, reassuring herself. "No way at all."

Diving deep and scattering purple fishes, she tried hard to shed her doubts, but they clung with tiny sharp claws and she knew they wouldn't leave her for a long, long time.

Giving up, she surged out of the ocean and walked back to the house, dripping water everywhere like a shaggy dog. "A nice long bath," she promised herself. "That'll take care of this."

But it didn't. Her mind was racing, full of him, of them . . . of Jimmy.

She winced, real pain coursing through her. She had to keep her distance from Ken Forrest. He must never, never know about Jimmy. Jimmy was all she had in this world and she wasn't going to risk losing him.

And there was something else. Something she'd been avoiding. Even now, it made her cringe to think of it. She'd seen something back there at Hiroshi's, out of the corner of her eye, when she'd spotted Ken mounting the steps. There had been people in the car he'd emerged from. A blond woman had been sitting in the front passenger seat, and two children had been in the back.

She made herself face that picture squarely as she entered her home and a huge ache began to grow inside her, pushing at her chest.

"No," she whispered, closing her eyes. No, she wouldn't think about that. What was the use? She was never going to see him again. There was no point in thinking about it.

Dressing quickly, she came out of her bedroom and then stopped cold, gasping in surprise. There was a man in her living room and for just a second...

But, no. It was only her cousin, Reggie. She scowled. "What are you doing here? I thought you had a new job in Honolulu."

He nodded his handsome silver head. "I did. But I gave it up. I've got a new idea."

She groaned, half laughing. Reggie's "ideas" were legendary in their family. "Oh, no. What now?"

His eyes were bright with excitement. New ideas always did that to him. "It's too good to just tell like this." He grinned at her, shrugging in his carefree way. "I'm so damn antsy, I can't sit still. Come have dinner with me, Shawnee. I need someone to talk to."

She hesitated. She didn't need to go in to work. Her place, the Paukai Café, was set up and running like a top. Jimmy was gone, visiting his uncle Mack on the other side of the island for a few days. And she needed to get out of the house. If she stayed here, she would obsess on the past and end up crying her eyes out. Better she should go out with Reggie.

"Okay," she decided quickly. "Just let me change into something a little fancier." She turned, pulling the band off her braided hair. "But I get to pick the restaurant, okay? None of that greasy fried food you always go for."

"Hey, what's wrong with the Sizzling Skipper?" he called after her, laughing.

Making a face at her cousin, she disappeared into her bedroom and let out a long sigh of relief. Reggie would keep her mind off Ken for the evening. And then she would get some sleep, and everything would be back to normal by morning. It had to be.

Ken sat alone at the table by the window and tried to relax. The room was filled with happy, chattering people, mostly couples. The decor was Pacific Island, the menu emphasized seafood. He was going to nurse a tall, cold drink and enjoy this time alone before ordering. He felt a twinge of guilt at how glad he was that Karen had decided to stay back at the hotel with the children, but he suppressed it. He needed some time alone. He wanted to remember.

He'd eaten here once before, seventeen years ago when he'd come back looking for the beautiful girl he'd fallen in love with that crazy summer. Just like this time, he hadn't found her. Quickly he scanned the faces in the restaurant, then had to laugh at himself.

He was living in a dreamworld, and he knew it. Even if he *did* find her, she would be married, have a passel of kids by now. He was searching for a past that didn't exist any longer and he was totally aware of that. He just didn't seem to be able to stop himself.

Funny how life got away from you. How could so many years have gone by already? How was it that he had never found an extra minute to come looking for that girl again in all this time? For one brief moment in space, she'd been everything to him. Now she was a memory, a recollection of a feeling he only wanted to feel once more.

Good Lord, he was beginning to sound like an old man— as though the main part of his life were over. Frowning, he leaned back in his seat and let his gaze drift over the other people in the room. But he didn't really see them. His mind was on his past, on the image of a lovely girl, her naked, cinnamon skin shimmering in the sunlight, her tawny hair floating around her like a cloud, her arms open, welcoming him. For just a moment, it was so real.

"Now isn't this nicer than your hole-in-the-wall grease joint?" Shawnee looked around the busy room and smiled, glad the mood was lively. She needed that.

"What have you got against the Skipper?" Reggie growled again. "The Skipper has history and tradition behind it."

Shawnee grinned at him, glad she'd come. She was feeling better already. "A tradition of bad taste and a history of food poisoning. Remember Uncle Toki?"

Reggie's handsome face registered outrage. "Hey, that's not fair. He could have eaten a bad fig or something before he ever showed up at the place that night."

She rolled her eyes. "He nearly died, Reggie."

"Yeah. And as soon as they released him from the hospital, where did he go? Right back to the Skipper's for french fries."

She sighed. "Giving rise to the rumor that there may be a streak of insanity in our family, after all," she murmured.

The hostess arrived before Reggie could think of a good retort to that one, and offered to show them to their table. Shawnee followed her, smiling her thanks as she turned to slide into the chair the hostess indicated. And out of the corner of her eye, as she slipped down into her seat, she thought she saw . . .

No. It couldn't be. She sat very still, feeling all the blood drain from her face. She couldn't turn and look. Her heart was beating too hard, and her face would show everything she was feeling.

Reggie sat down and looked at her curiously. "What's the matter?" he asked, leaning toward her.

"Nothing," she said in a tiny voice, shaking her head. Not listening as he began to talk, she tried to think. Was she just dreaming? That had to be it. She was obsessing on this thing and she'd imagined she saw him sitting there. If she turned around now and just took a look . . .

She couldn't do it. It *was* him. She could feel it. And if she turned and looked, she would have to acknowledge his presence.

His presence. Oh, Lord. She closed her eyes and tried to keep her breathing steady.

"Hey." Reggie leaned close again, staring at her pale face. "What is the matter with you?" he demanded.

She shook her head once more and looked at him, wanting to shut him up but not knowing how to do it without making it obvious.

His eyes narrowed with a sure instinct. "Is it one of those woman things?" he asked sympathetically.

She frowned and tried to understand what he was saying. She could hardly hear his words with this roaring in her ears. "What 'woman things'?" she mumbled.

Reggie shrugged. "I don't know. Women are mysterious creatures."

She took a deep breath and tried to smile. "Women are very down-to-earth, common sense creatures," she countered, squaring her shoulders and lifting her chin, giving herself a pep talk as much as answering him. She could do this thing. All she had to do was remain strong and not give in to panic. "It's men who live in a dreamworld."

Reggie gave her a slashing grin. "I suppose you think that way of your son Jimmy?"

"Jimmy is...different." She lowered her voice and leaned closer to her cousin. "I love Jimmy." She had to stop herself from taking an automatic glance over her shoulder to see if he was listening.

Listening! This was crazy, purely insane. She was just being paranoid. He wasn't back there. He couldn't be. And even if he were, he probably hadn't seen her, or he would have said something by now. No, he couldn't be there. She would have to go on that assumption and hope for the best.

But she wished Reggie hadn't said Jimmy's name so loudly. Jimmy was her secret. Ken must never, never know.

The waiter set glasses of water on the table and she drank hers thirstily, settling herself. It was nuts to think Ken was sitting at the table behind her—just her imagination working overtime. She was going to calm down and enjoy this dinner. Taking a deep breath, she tried to focus on what Reggie was saying.

"...And we'll spend most of our time in those rubber rafts you blow up. You know what I mean?"

She blinked at him, finally tuning him back in and utterly at sea as to what he was talking about.

"We'll camouflage the rafts with moss and seaweed and stuff. We'll look like floating islands."

His handsome face was animated with excitement and she realized he must be going over his new idea.

Reggie's ideas usually involved asking her for money. Though he was just about the same age as she was, she'd always felt like an older sister to him. Sometimes she lent him the cash, sometimes she told him he was off the beam. He took either result with his usual good-natured smile.

That was what made it hard to turn him down, though. He was truly a lovable guy.

"We'll lie down on the bottoms with just our eyes peeking over the sides—" he bent his head down as though he were scrunching down in the raft at that very moment, shifting his eyes back and forth and grimacing "—while we let the rafts float in and out among the rocks...." He waved the flat of his hand around, illustrating his point.

She blinked. He'd lost her. "Reggie, what on earth are you talking about?"

His dark eyes were wide and innocent. "The mermaids. We'll drift out at night and..."

"Mermaids?" She shook her head, not sure she'd heard right. "What mermaids?"

Reggie was beginning to grow impatient with her. "I just got through telling you. Weren't you listening? The documentary I'm filming. The mermaids of Hamakua Point. I'm going to catch them on film."

She stared at her cousin. Somehow in the time her mind had been off on the old days with Ken Forrest, the earth had taken a sharp turn to the left and she'd missed it. She shook her head, getting equilibrium back. "Reggie," she said slowly, studying his eager face, "you can't get mermaids on film. You can't film things that don't really exist."

He laughed with light scorn. "Of course not. I know that. But these are the mermaids of Hamakua Point," he said seriously, as though that settled the matter.

Shawnee stared at him for another moment, then smiled and patted his arm. "They don't exist," she repeated.

Reggie grinned, shaking his head as though she were just the cutest thing. "I knew you would say that. But I'm going to prove they do." He drummed his fingers on the table, providing a drumroll to his zinger. "Remember that picture of the Loch Ness Monster in all the magazines?"

"That grainy black and white that looked like a drainpipe in a puddle?"

His offended look let her know that photography of paranormal items and experiences was not a subject for humor at the moment. "It may have been grainy, but it proved the monster existed. And it set a precedent. Now, I'm going to prove the mermaids exist, too."

He was serious. She could hardly believe it. Laughing softly, she said, "Reggie, it's just a legend."

He shrugged. "Where do you think legends come from? They don't just pop into people's heads, you know. They've gotta be based in fact somewhere along the line."

She shook her head, nonplussed. How was she going to talk him out of this one? That was her job, after all—trying to save him from making an utter fool of himself. "Remember the time I helped you buy those strange chickens?"

He looked hurt that she was bringing up failures from the past. "That was supposed to work. They were supposed to lay blue eggs. I was going to make a killing that Easter."

"Well, they didn't lay blue eggs."

"Those eggs they laid weren't white," he said, as though that scored one for his side.

"No, they weren't white," she agreed. "But they weren't any color anyone wanted to see in their Easter basket, either." She patted his arm again. "And remember the time you tried to sell refrigerators door-to-door? Or how about the time you started that magazine, *Matchmaking for Your Pet?*"

He shook his head, dismissing those ancient examples of great ideas that just hadn't made it. "But those were *old* ideas, Shawnee. This is a new one. This will work."

Oh, brother. How was she going to get through to him?

"Reggie, if you want to make a video documentary on something, why don't you do it on Pirate Morgan Caine?"

Reggie grimaced. "Our old ancestor? Who would be interested in that old geezer?"

"I think it's a very interesting story, how he got blown off course and how he married the Polynesian princess and everything."

"I can never remember if he's our great-great-great-grandfather or our great-great-great-*great* . . ."

"Whatever. He still seems to influence the lives of all his offspring."

"Right. His legacy is like a curse. We're all doomed."

She laughed. There had been times she'd felt that way herself. Every streak of wildness in the Caines was always attributed to the genetic influence of the pirate. It was said he was only happy when his progeny was incorrigible. He hated ordinary lives.

She'd wondered now and then if it was his bloodline that had made her do what she'd done all those years ago. But that was silly. And it was far too easy to throw the blame on something else.

"I might consider doing a documentary on him someday," Reggie was musing dreamily, "but right now I've got to go with my gut feeling. And my gut tells me—mermaids!"

Who could throw cold water on such innocent faith? Shawnee stared into his eyes for a long moment, then laughed softly. "Okay, Reggie," she said, surrendering to the inevitable. "Tell me all about it."

He'd had too many tall cold ones. It was time to order some dinner and get back to the hotel. Getting soused wasn't going to help anything. And it wasn't usually his way.

Depression and introspection in general were not his way. He was usually too busy to spend a lot of time thinking about anything but his work. The last few days had been the laziest he'd spent in years—probably since that summer so long ago.

Work had filled his life for much too long and he knew it, but he didn't know what the alternative was. Work ran in his family, it seemed. His brother Gary had worked like a madman up to the day he'd died in January. Gary had loved his work in real estate. The world was a giant Monopoly board to him, and he'd wanted to own Park Place. The trouble was, he hadn't collected enough of those little cards to save him from danger. One day he was gleefully buying and selling properties, the next he was dead.

Ken stretched in his chair, suddenly uncomfortable. He supposed it was true that his brother's death had made him reexamine his own life. Why not? It seemed the logical thing to do. He loved his legal practice almost as much as Gary had loved realty, but there had always been a part of him that knew there was something more out there—something lacking in his life—something he'd caught a glimpse of that summer.

He glanced around the room again and his gaze fell on a new couple a few tables away. The woman was sitting with her back to him and his imagination was immediately captured by her long, beautiful hair. It fell in a rich, silky wave, like chocolate cream, catching golden sparks from the lights. He indulged himself, staring at it through narrowed eyes, remembering *her* hair and how it had just touched her shoulders, but had been just as lush, just as shiny—

His hands went cold. From out of nowhere it came to him. This could be her.

No, he told himself, throwing back his head and trying to pull his gaze away. It's not her, you jerk. It couldn't be her. She would be older now, more sophisticated. She wouldn't wear her hair that way.

But his heart was thumping so hard he could barely breathe. What if it was her? What if she were sitting just a few feet away from him? What if it was just that easy to reach out and pluck back the past?

Okay, she was better now. She'd settled down. She knew that couldn't possibly be Ken Forrest behind her. That would be just too many coincidences in one day. She was just hypersensitive because she had seen him that afternoon at Hiroshi's. Probably he was off at some touristy restaurant enjoying some overpriced nouveau pickings with his blond wife and his two children. Probably he was thinking about packing up and catching a plane back to Honolulu in the morning. Probably she didn't have a thing to worry about.

"Hey, you want to dance?"

Reggie loved to dance. It was one of his most endearing qualities. And, on most occasions, Shawnee loved to indulge him.

"I don't know," she said doubtfully.

"Come on. They're playing a tango. You do a great tango."

She grinned. She did love to dance with him. But then a tremor ran through her, just a tiny premonition...

"Not a tango, Reggie. If they play a slow one after this, I'll dance with you."

The music changed. The tango gave way to a moody piece just right for dancing cheek-to-cheek. Reggie pushed back his chair, and she sighed. She was going to have to get up and go with him.

Her pulse began to flutter. She was going to have to face the man behind her and see if it was him or not. She was quite sure it wasn't, but just in case... She squared her shoulders and took a deep breath, then let Reggie help push back her chair. She was standing. She was turning. In a moment, she would be looking right at him. Yes. There he was. And then the bottom fell out of her soul. *It was him.*

TWO

It was her. Without realizing what he was doing, he rose from his chair, staring right into her eyes. She was so beautiful, hardly changed at all. Her hair seemed to fly around her like a magical cloak, catching the warm glow of the candles on the tables around them. Her rich, green eyes drew him in, held him. They were wide with shock.

He couldn't speak. He wanted to say something, reach for her, but he couldn't. It was as though there was something between them—time, space, memories—and he couldn't get beyond that. But their eyes still held. It seemed to take forever for her to turn completely and look at him. And then he felt as though he were drifting toward her, already lost in her embrace, even though he hadn't moved at all. She was real. She was here. Everything he'd been dreaming for years had come to pass. All he had to do was reach for her and...

Then, incredibly, she was turning away. He still couldn't do anything. He couldn't move. He stood, paralyzed, staring after her as she let herself fall into the arms of a tall, silver-haired man who was leading her to the center of the dance floor. They began to dance. Her eyes were closed. They swayed together, and she never looked back, not even for a moment.

He couldn't believe it. Was he really still dreaming? Was she really real?

He couldn't think anything through. He could only act on instinct. That was the only cognitive process that still seemed to be connected to anything workable in his brain. Slowly he walked toward the dance floor. Slowly he moved toward her.

She didn't look, but she could sense him coming toward them. What on earth was she going to do? She couldn't let him close. She had to protect herself. Clutching her cousin with flexed fingers, she whispered a plea.

"Reggie, quick. Pretend we're married. You're my husband."

"Your husband!" The horror on his handsome face would have been insulting if she'd had the time and presence of mind to notice.

"Yes, quickly. There's somebody here..."

He pulled away and looked down at her. "I can't do that. Isn't that incest or something?"

Reggie was a dear, but not fast enough on the uptake for things like this. Still, he was her only hope. "We're only cousins. It's okay. I think it's even legal in some states."

"I doubt it." He shuddered delicately. "Hey, Shawnee, I love you and everything, but this gives me the creeps."

Creeps or no, it was all she had to work with. Ken was almost upon them, just about to make contact with her and force her to acknowledge their past. She could feel him. "Please," she begged Reggie in a hoarse whisper. "Just pretend."

And then she held her breath and waited.

*   *   *

He felt as though he were moving in a dream, moving through mist, but as he got closer, the mist began to melt away. She was real, all right. She'd seen him coming. She'd noticed him out of the corner of her eye. He could see the flush beginning to creep up her cheeks.

"Shawnee," he said softly, just a few feet away.

She stopped dead in her tracks, but didn't turn.

"Shawnee. Don't you remember me?"

Finally she turned and stared at him. "I—I'm not sure," she said awkwardly, but he knew she was lying. Her eyes were wide and full of trepidation. He smiled, confidence flowing back.

"It's no good, Shawnee. You remember. I know you do."

She blinked those beautiful green eyes and the corners of her mouth tilted a bit. It was almost a smile. "Ken Forrest, isn't it?" she said in a faint voice.

A light gleamed in his blue black eyes. "That's right."

"It's been a long time," she murmured.

He held out his hand, a bridge from the past. "Dance with me," he said.

"I..." She looked at Reggie, her eyes pleading for help.

But he'd seen the look on Ken's face. He raised his hands and shook his head ruefully. "What do you want me to do?" he mouthed to her.

She gave up. "Just for the rest of this song," she said grudgingly, and Reggie went back to the table quite happily.

She must have said something after that, but she wasn't sure what. All she knew was what she saw in the depths of Ken's eyes, and then his arms were sliding around her and she was floating. She didn't feel as though she were breathing at all.

He couldn't say anything. It was very strange. There was a lump in his throat. He held her lightly, but he wanted to crush her to his chest. There was a powerful emotion surging inside him and he wasn't sure what it was going to do, so he simply rode it, like a wave in the surf.

She was trembling deep inside. She hoped he couldn't feel it. She didn't want him to know. It was just a reaction to the memories, after all. Nothing to worry about. Just as long as she didn't faint.

The music seemed to go on and on, and when it finally faded, he didn't let go right away. She wanted desperately to get away from him, run somewhere he couldn't hold her, couldn't touch her like this. Being with him had once been a dream. Right now, it was a nightmare.

Finally she slipped out of his arms and he let her go. Reluctantly she looked up into his eyes. Smile, she ordered herself silently. He had to think she was treating this encounter as casually as possible. If he thought anything else, she would be in trouble.

"Thanks," she chirped, her voice higher than usual, sounding shrill in her ears. "Gee, it's been nice seeing you again. I suppose you're here on vacation?"

He nodded, his dark lashes shadowing his eyes. "Sort of," he said. And his shoulders loosened, relaxing. If she could smile, he could, too.

"Well, I hope you have a nice trip," she said quickly, looking around. "I guess I'd better get back to Reggie."

Ken turned and looked at her table, frowning. "Is he your date?" he asked shortly.

She took a deep breath and pasted the smile very firmly on her face. "I . . . he . . . we're married." She glanced away and coughed, and made herself smile again.

"You married *him?*" Ken stared at Reggie as though that couldn't be possible. "Are you sure?"

She jerked a bit defensively, wishing she were a better liar. "Marriage is one of those things you tend to remember."

Her chin rose. "I'm so sorry if you don't approve," she said dryly.

"Oh, no, I..." He shrugged, looking befuddled. "I'm sorry, it's just that..." His eyes softened, deepened. Reaching out, he touched her hair with one finger. "I guess I don't like to think of you married," he said softly.

She let herself look deeply into his eyes and immediately knew it was a big mistake. A woman could lose herself in all that velvet blueness.

"I—I'd better get back to Reggie," she managed to murmur, twisting away.

"Wait." His hand was on her arm. "We need to talk."

"Why?" She pulled away from him, stepping back so he wasn't so close.

He stared at her. Her green eyes were so cool, so level, as though she didn't have a single emotion in her body. Couldn't she sense the storm that was raging through his veins? Didn't she remember how it had felt when they'd been together before? Didn't she want to remember?

"It would be fun to talk over old times."

She glanced away, avoiding his eyes, and started toward the table. He came along beside her, as she had known he would. But she was heading for sanctuary. It wasn't often that Reggie looked like a beacon of hope.

"That was all a long time ago," she said as she walked. "There's been a lot of water under the bridge since then. We were so young, I hardly remember."

Hardly remember? He felt a flash of outrage. How could she not remember something that still lived inside him as though it had happened yesterday? "You don't remember?" he repeated, incredulous.

She managed to keep her gaze cool. "Well, hardly."

Despite her demeanor, he was sure she was bluffing. His grin was lopsided and he caught hold of her arm, pulling her close again. "Then let me remind you," he said.

Her eyes blazed. "Let go of me," she demanded, yanking out of his grasp. "I don't need to be reminded of anything."

He released her, but he didn't apologize. "Shawnee," he said softly, "how is it possible that you're even more beautiful today?"

She avoided his gaze, her heart thumping in her chest, and started moving through the room again, wishing she knew how to shake him. They reached the table and Reggie smiled, standing to greet them.

"Hey, listen," he said genially, the perfect host, "why don't you join us?"

Shawnee almost gasped aloud, but her cousin didn't notice. He grinned at Ken as though he'd known him forever, as though he couldn't wait to get his views on just about everything.

"You and Shawnee are obviously old friends. I'm sure you've got a lot to talk about."

Ken glanced at Shawnee, triumph in the curve of his mouth. He knew she was trying to avoid him. What he didn't know was why.

"Well, thank you. I'd love to join you." He held out Shawnee's chair for her, then turned. "Just a moment. I'll get my drink and be back."

He turned and was gone, and Shawnee glared at Reggie as he sat across from her. "What did you do that for?" she asked, just barely keeping panic at bay. "I told you I wanted to keep him away."

Reggie looked surprised, as though he'd forgotten all that. "Hey, he's a nice guy. You can see that." He frowned speculatively. "I've got this feeling I've seen him some place before, you know? He looks so darn familiar."

Shawnee felt cold. Of course. How could she have forgotten? Ken looked so very much like Jimmy, anyone who knew him was bound to notice the resemblance. All she could do now was pray that Reggie wouldn't make the connection and blurt it out at the table.

But Reggie's attention had gone on to other things. "Hey, he looks like a man with money. Think he might want to get in on the action with my mermaid project?"

Could this get any worse? Her shoulders sank. "Reggie, don't you dare."

Reggie didn't understand this sort of reticence. To him, the world was full of friends. "You don't mind if I just sort of outline it to him, do you? You never know. He might be interested."

What he was, was almost back. She turned so Ken couldn't see her lips and whispered, "Don't you say a word. And remember, we're married."

Ken reached the table and pulled out the chair nearest Shawnee, dropping into it with athletic ease and smiling at the two of them. She gave him a fleeting smile in return, then concentrated on the drink sitting before her, wrapping her fingers around the icy surface and staring down into the golden depths. She wasn't going to make conversation. He was the one who had wanted to sit here. He was going to have to take care of the entertainment, if he wanted any.

But she'd overlooked Reggie. No silence could last long with her cousin nearby. Reggie started on a discourse about local politics, and Shawnee had a moment to study Ken covertly while he pretended to be interested in what Reggie was saying.

His handsome face had hardened. Where there had once been dimples, deep grooves outlined his mouth. The nose was large, with a higher arch than she'd remembered. And the eyes were even more penetrating than ever, bright with a clear intelligence, almost sharp, as though he could see into things people were trying to hide. She felt a tiny shiver as she thought that. She would have to keep from meeting his gaze as much as possible.

He'd been a blonde when she'd known him before. Now his hair had darkened, but there were still streaks of sun in it. He probably played golf, she thought dismissively. With clients. Or judges. His life had taken a very different turn from hers. But it was just as well. They'd never been a match made in heaven. She'd always known that.

Looking up, she met his gaze and realized he was giving her the once-over, too. She couldn't read the evaluation he'd come to in his eyes. Had she changed? She felt like a different woman. But of course, that was the point. Now, she was a woman. Then, she'd been a girl.

"Well, Shawnee, what have you been up to all these years?" he asked, obviously trying to draw her into the conversation.

"Life," she said shortly, determined to let him know she wasn't happy to have him sitting with them. "This and that. How about you?"

"Me?" He looked almost surprised to be asked. "Nothing very interesting I'm afraid."

She glanced at him and then away. "Did you go to college? And law school?"

Aha. He swallowed a grin. So she did remember, after all. "Yes, I did both those things. And I've been practicing law ever since."

Her mouth twisted cynically. "You're probably a senior partner in your firm by now. Right? Handling all the most important cases?"

He hesitated. That was a very perceptive description of exactly where he stood, but somehow, in her voice, it sounded like a condemnation rather than a compliment. So he nodded, but changed the subject.

"So you two are married, are you?"

Funny how they both looked up at him, startled. He smiled to himself. His instincts didn't lie. There was something fishy going on here.

"How long have you been married?" he probed, going for it.

"Years and years," Shawnee said quickly.

"Oh, not too long," Reggie said at the same time. They glanced at each other, Reggie in chagrin, Shawnee in horror.

Ken forced back the grin that threatened to give him away. "I suppose it's a matter of perspective," he said doubtfully, his wide mouth twisting as he looked from one to the other. "Do you have any children?"

Reggie threw out his arms expansively, obviously wanting to make up for his previous error. "Kids? We got 'em. Tons of 'em. Kids galore. Why, we've got boys and we've got girls and we've got..." He paused, frowning, thinking hard for one more category.

Shawnee gave him a hard, stabbing kick under the table. This charade was crumbling before her eyes. There was no way he was going to think up a third gender, no matter how hard he tried.

"Reggie exaggerates a little," she said quickly, her cool eyes defying Ken not to believe her explanation.

Then she deliberately changed the subject herself. "Your glass is almost empty. Would you like me to call the waitress? It looks like your drink needs freshening." She tried a sunny smile, but the cynical glint didn't leave his dark blue eyes for a moment.

"I'm just fine, thanks," he drawled, looking her over. Something sharp flashed behind the wall of his response. "But to get back to you two... something I just noticed." His smile was bleak. "It seems rather odd, but maybe it's just the custom here. Neither one of you is wearing a wedding ring."

They both glanced involuntarily at their hands and reddened. Shawnee's throat was dry and she was wondering why she had ever thought she could get away with this. But Reggie wasn't about to give up.

"That's right," he said stoutly. "We've got 'em at the jewelers. They're...uh...they're being cleaned."

Ken's mouth twisted and one eyebrow rose. "Cleaned?"

Reggie blinked as though to say, Was that wrong? "Uh, no, I mean, they're being reshaped," he amended hastily.

Now both eyebrows rose. "Reshaped?"

Shawnee shook her head, feeling numb. It was no use. Reggie meant well, but he was nothing short of disaster as a conspirator.

"I don't know," Reggie said, losing hope, his eyes huge with sorrow that he'd muffed this. "They're doing something fancy to 'em. Aren't they, Shawnee?"

Reaching out, she squeezed his hand. "It's okay," she began, ready to fess up. But before she could get started, Reggie had a new idea.

"I know what," he interjected brightly. "I hawked 'em to get money for my project." Reggie grinned in triumph. "That's where they are."

Shawnee wanted to hide her face in her hands. "Oh, Reggie," she murmured, half laughing.

"Sure. Why not?"

She looked at Ken. His eyes were sparkling with laughter. He was having none of it, that much was obvious. She shrugged. All she wanted was to get this horrible evening over with.

"You know, it's getting late. I suppose we should order some food," she said desperately. "You haven't eaten yet, I take it?"

Ken glanced at his watch. It was already over an hour later than he'd told Karen he would be. She would be worried, he knew that well enough. He hesitated. He didn't want to leave Shawnee now that he'd found her. But he couldn't leave Karen hanging.

"I don't really have enough time to eat," he said. "I'm going to have to get going."

Relief swept through Shawnee, making her almost light-headed. "Oh. That's too bad," she murmured, but she couldn't hold back the smile.

Ken looked at Shawnee, reading her like a book. He still didn't have a clue as to why she was so ready to pretend they'd never had the relationship that had once trans-formed the two of them. He had to find out why. And he had to find out more—where she lived, when he could see her again.

"Will you dance with me one more time?" he asked.

She hesitated. He was going. That was the important thing. She would lay low for the next few days, just in case, and make sure he didn't make contact again. And then, surely, he would be winging his way home and this ordeal would be over. She would have to dance with him one more time. But after that, it would be over.

"Of course," she said, exhilarated at the prospect of his leaving.

He stood and helped her to her feet. They walked slowly to the dance floor, and his arms came around her again. She closed her eyes, hardening herself—or trying to. There was a melting sensation going on in her body. She didn't seem to be able to stop it. His fingers brushing her neck, his warm breath stirring her hair, the sense of his heartbeat so close to her face—it was all too much. Her skin was tingling and her breath was coming much too fast.

No, she had to fight this. Forcing herself, she stiffened, holding herself aloof, forsaking grace for armor.

He felt her reserve and wondered if this was just the way she was these days, or if this remoteness was just for him. He remembered a woman with a body as warm and pliant as wax in the sun. Where had that woman gone? Could she really have changed that much?

Well, if she wouldn't dance with him, she would have to talk. "Why are you pretending to be married to Reggie?" he asked her abruptly.

She looked up, a little stunned and working hard not to show it. "How do you know I'm pretending?" she countered without much hope of convincing anyone.

"Any fool can see the two of you aren't married."

She stared into his eyes and finally, she shrugged. "I don't really care what you believe to be true," she murmured, looking away.

His grip on her tightened with his impatience. "You pretend to be married, you pretend you don't remember me. What's going on, Shawnee?"

She met his gaze with a level one of her own. "Did it ever occur to you that I might not want to dredge up the past?" she asked calmly. "You come bounding into my life as though you have a right to be there. But you don't, Ken. We have nothing real between us."

Her cool tone startled him almost as much as the words she used. "Nothing real?" he repeated, marveling at how she could look at that past so differently from the way he did.

"That's right. You were a tourist, Ken. We get a lot of tourists here. They come and they go. We don't change. You came and you went. Now you're back again." She held her tone steady, even though there were tears threatening in her heart. There was a time when she had wept for days over this very fact. "Big deal. In another day or two, you'll be gone."

Ken stared down at her, barely moving his feet. "But I'm here now, Shawnee," he said softly. "Can't we be together?"

Be together? She searched his eyes, wondering what he really meant, pretty sure she knew. "No," she said simply. "I've got my life. And you've got yours."

He smiled. He actually had the nerve to smile. "But mine would be so much richer with you in it," he said. "You were my first love, you know."

She had to fight hard not to take that at face value. He didn't really mean it. It was all a line.

Besides, he wasn't saying anything about the blonde in the car, or the two kids she'd seen. Was he going to pretend they didn't exist? Anger burned in her heart. This was no good. It wasn't going to work. He wasn't being straight with her.

"That was a long time ago. And we barely knew each other. Less than a week."

He cupped her cheek with his hand. "Less than a week. It's true. And you changed my life."

She drew back, pushing his hand away. "*I* changed *your* life?" If he only knew. She closed her eyes for a moment.

"I was a boy when I came to Hawaii. I felt like a man when I left."

Her eyes snapped open and she glared at him. "Did you?" Anger flashed through her in sparks. Of all the arrogant jerks she'd ever met. What did he want to do, pin a little gold ribbon on her chest for being his first sexual experience? What an honor. "Better than Disneyland, huh?" she muttered, looking away.

"What?" he asked, not sure he'd heard her correctly.

"Nothing." She pulled out of his arms and took a step backward. "I'm going to the ladies' room, Ken. I'm going to powder my nose. When I come out, you'd better be gone. Because if you're not, *I'll* leave."

He gazed at her, bewildered. She started to turn, but he grabbed her arm, forcing her to hear one last thing. "Shawnee," he said slowly, savoring the name as though it had taste as well as sound. "You escaped me the last time I came looking for you. I knew I'd find you this time. And I'm not about to let you go this easily."

She turned and held his gaze. "Did it ever occur to you that it might not be your choice?" she asked.

And then she left him, walking with her head held high, until she was out of sight around the corner. Once behind the gold and white door to the rest rooms she took a step and then she crumpled, sinking into a chair before the long mirror, holding her head in her hands.

She wasn't going to cry. She bit back the tears and clenched her jaw fiercely. There was nothing to cry over. Ken was the past, a dream that had bothered her one more time. Now it was over. That was all there was to it.

It took a few minutes to restore her composure, but when she emerged, Ken wasn't in sight. She walked carefully to the table where Reggie was sitting, playing drums with the silverware.

"Is he gone?" she asked cautiously.

"Like the wind," Reggie responded. "Sit down. Let's eat."

She stood where she was and looked down at him. "You didn't tell him where I live, did you?"

Reggie stopped and looked up at her. "He didn't ask *that*," he said, and waited with trepidation in his eyes for the question that would surely follow.

But Shawnee didn't notice. She was looking toward the doorway. "Good," she said, and Reggie heaved a sigh of relief.

"He was a nice guy. I don't know why you're acting so weird about him."

"I'm not acting weird. Just . . . careful."

Reggie had no patience with analyzing relationships. He shrugged it away. "Let's eat," he repeated, looking around for the waitress.

She glanced down. "No, I'm much too wound up to eat. I think I'd better get home. You can stay if you like."

Reggie sighed, his eyes mournful. "No, no. I'll drive you."

"Thanks." She smiled at him as he rose to join her, throwing a large bill on the table. He was such a dear, despite everything, and she wanted to get that sad look off his face. "That way you can stop at the Skipper's on your way home," she reminded him.

"Hey." Joy returned to his eyes. "You're right."

She had to laugh, slipping her arm through his. "Thanks for everything, cousin," she told him as they left the building for the parking lot. "You were a big help tonight."

"You mean that being married stuff?" He frowned. "Think he bought it?" he asked doubtfully.

"Oh, absolutely," she told him, chuckling. "No doubt about it."

Three

—

She actually did consider hiding out at home for a few days, just in case. The restaurant could surely run just fine without her. But Pilani had called in a panic over a doughnut crisis in the morning, and she'd had to go in to straighten things out. Once she was there, it didn't seem to make any sense to run back home to hide.

Besides, Ken didn't know about her café. If he were looking for her at all, he was most likely looking in the wrong corner of the island. She didn't live there anymore. And how could he possibly know where she was now? Her name wasn't in the phone book, and there was no one to tell him. Now if she didn't run around on the roads too much, maybe she could avoid him altogether.

She had to shake her head when she realized what she was doing. She was hiding—hiding from Ken, the man she had once prayed would come back to her. Now he was back and she was scared to death of him.

She'd made it through the evening before without too big a disaster. It was too bad he still looked so good and seemed so much the same. The same qualities that had captured her heart eighteen years ago were still at work, and she was still susceptible. That was why she couldn't let herself think about him too much. She had to keep up the steel wall she'd built around her heart. If she let go, even for just a moment, she wasn't sure what might happen.

The breakfast crowd was beginning to thin out when a slim girl of about sixteen came in, blinking in the dim lights. Her dark brown hair was cut short, giving her a tomboyish appearance. Jeans and an oversize T-shirt completed the picture.

"Excuse me," she said, looking Shawnee straight in the eye. "Are you Shawnee Caine?"

Shawnee paused, a trayful of plates overflowing with waffles in her hands, and smiled. The girl was probably looking for a job, but somehow she didn't look the type to waitress. "I sure am. What can I do for you?"

"You're Jimmy's mother, right?"

Shawnee lowered the tray. Aha. Another one of Jimmy's many fans. Ever since junior high, girls had seemed to gather wherever her son happened to be. And on the days Jimmy worked for her here in the restaurant, the clientele seemed to tilt decidedly to the feminine side. "Yes, I'm his mother," she admitted. "But he's not here right now."

"Oh."

Shawnee had to smile. The girl was trying hard to hide her disappointment, but it was a lost cause.

"Well, I didn't really come to see him," she said quickly. "Actually, your cousin, Reggie Caine, is meeting me here."

Shawnee frowned, then turned and snagged Pilani, who was passing by. She handed off the tray, so that she could be free to find out what was going on here.

"Come on over and sit down," she said to the girl, leading her to a small table near the kitchen. "And tell me what this is all about."

The girl sat down and looked around the room, slightly nervous, but making a brave attempt at exhibiting a self-confidence she obviously didn't really feel. It made Shawnee smile again.

"What's your name?" she asked her.

"Oh." The girl started in her seat. "I'm sorry. The name is Lani Tanaka. I know Jimmy from . . . friends. Oh, and I know your brother Mack. I work on his plane sometimes."

"Do you?" Shawnee's smile widened into a friendly grin. "He's a great guy, isn't he?" She sobered. "But, tell me, just why are you meeting my cousin here?" she asked her.

"I'm applying for a job with him."

Shawnee stared. "A job? With Reggie?"

Lani nodded, her eyes bright. "He says he needs someone to help him film a documentary."

Shawnee gasped. "Oh, no, he's got you roped into this?"

"It's going to be great." Lani's face shone with the light of one who'd definitely been won over to the project. "He's got some great ideas for it."

What could she do? Give the girl a rundown on all Reggie's past failures and break her heart? "You do know what he's planning to document, don't you?" she tried skeptically.

The dark eyes didn't blink. "Sure. The mermaids of Hamakua Point."

"Right. Have you ever seen any mermaids at Hamakua Point?"

"No, but . . ."

Shawnee sighed. "Neither has anyone else, Lani. It's just a legend."

"I know. But . . ."

She leaned forward earnestly. "Lani, you're going to spend hours and hours in the hot sun on the bottom of a rubber raft, peering over the side with a video camera, and catching nothing but screaming sea gulls and leaping dolphins."

"I know." She looked so earnest. "But that could all be in the documentary, too."

Shawnee shook her head. Reggie was obviously a much better salesperson than she was. He had a convert here. Funny, the girl looked too intelligent to fall for it. Well, she'd tried. Now it was up to Lani to make her own decisions.

"Uh..." Lani leaned forward, a slight flush on her cheeks. "Do you think Jimmy will be around tomorrow when we start? Your cousin said he might be helping, too."

So that was it. She wasn't really falling for it, after all. She had ulterior motives. Shawnee smothered a grin, and shrugged.

"There's no telling what that boy will get himself into," she said, sighing. Poor girl. Shawnee liked the look of her, but she certainly wasn't the type Jimmy usually fell for these days. Nothing at all like the very fancy Misty he was seeing right now—she of the skintight leather mini skirts and four-inch heels. It was too bad.

Jimmy was a good boy, but lately his taste in friends had taken a turn for the worst. That worried her, but Misty worried her even more. She knew only too well the temptations of being a teenager. She would do almost anything to make sure her son didn't ruin his life.

It would be nice if Jimmy could fall for a girl like this Lani. She looked like a girl with a head on her shoulders—even if she *was* working for Reggie. But there wasn't much hope of that. Ever since junior high, girls had chased Jimmy, and the ones who usually caught him weren't candidates for honors courses at the university.

Reggie came in and she left the two of them together to talk over details of hiring. And she went back to watching the door. She'd been on pins and needles all morning, worrying that every man who came in would turn out to be Ken, wishing the time would pass more quickly. She'd had about enough of that. Once she got the lunch details settled, she gave out instructions to her staff and decided to head for home and have a swim.

"Jimmy?" she called as she entered the house, even though his car wasn't in the drive and she knew he probably wasn't there. He wasn't due back until nightfall, at least, and she was thinking about calling and telling him to stay longer. But in the back of her mind was the fear that he would be back already, and that Ken would show up. "Jimmy?" she called again.

No answer. Good. She was alone.

The silky, electric blue one-piece fit her like a second skin. Quickly braiding her hair, she grabbed a towel and ran for the shore.

She had to swim, she had to swim hard and long and fast to try to shake the picture of Ken that burned in her like a curse. The water felt heavenly and she swam fiercely, out to the island and back, trying to rid herself of Ken's face, of his touch.

But it didn't help. In fact, things were getting worse, as though a storm were brewing and she could sense it. She had to stay away from him. There was no telling what would happen if he found out about Jimmy. And what if he and Jimmy came face to face?

One look at Jimmy's face and Ken would know. She couldn't let that happen. She couldn't let them see each other.

And there was another thing to consider. One look at Ken's face and *Jimmy* would know. How would she explain to her son that the father he thought had died years ago was very much alive and standing before him?

She had to stop and catch her breath, not because of hard swimming, but because she was so afraid. She'd once heard someone say that fear made every sense in the body come alive and that was the way she felt right now. She was practically jumping out of her skin. She could hardly stand it. Staying at work would have been better than this. At least there, she was only nervous. Here, she was going crazy.

Treading water, she looked out toward the open sea. There had been a time she'd thrown flowers out there, beyond the reef, wishing she could believe in the legend that doing so would bring Ken back. That legend hadn't been any truer than the one about the mermaids at Hamakua Point. Lei after lei had floated out to sea and Ken had not returned.

But wait a minute. He *had* come back. A little late, but here he was.

"Sorry, Ken," she whispered to the breeze. "It's too late. You missed the daddy due date."

But that didn't close off her heart. It couldn't. And she couldn't stop remembering how it had felt in his arms as they'd swayed to the music the night before. Her body had come alive as it hadn't done in years and years. If only things were different. If only the past wasn't between them. If only... if only he weren't married.

The knife really twisted in her chest on that thought. She'd been trying to ignore that picture in her mind of the blonde and the two children, but suddenly it was there, clear as a bell. And with it came a surge of anger that threatened to choke her. How dare he have another family! How dare he have a wife and children! How dare he smother those children with love when he had never so much as held Jimmy?

Had he been there to hear their first cries? Had he taught the boy to ride a bike? Did he play catch with him during baseball season? Did he carry him on his shoulders to watch the parade? Well, he hadn't done any of those things for Jimmy.

It wasn't fair. Tears came burning to her eyes. It wasn't fair that those children had so much and Jimmy had never had anything. She swam hard toward the reef, trying to shuck away the self-pity that had wrapped itself around her. She had to get rid of it before it ate her alive.

She was halfway back when she saw a man standing on the beach. She knew right away who it was. Her heartbeat seemed to fill the sky and echo from the horizon to the cliffs behind her house.

She didn't bother to worry about how he'd found her. She'd known it was inevitable, despite all her protestations to the contrary. She'd been expecting this all day. And now, here he was.

Rising slowly from the water, she walked toward him, staring straight into his eyes until she got to within a few feet, and then she stood, dripping and shivering slightly.

"Go away," she said simply. "Please."

He stared back and slowly shook his head. He'd never seen anything more beautiful, more exotic in his life. She was wet and shining in the sunlight, her body full and rounded but firm beneath the electric blue bit of cloth. Water dripped from her breasts and her nipples stood out sharply. The smooth lines of her legs, the neat indentation at her waist, the wide hips, all combined to flood him with a rush of desire such as he'd never felt before. He felt drunk, intoxicated on the sight of her.

"No," he said, just as she'd known he would.

She sighed, the fight seeping away. "All right, then come on in while I change."

Sweeping up her towel, she strode quickly toward the house. He came more slowly, savoring the sight of her. How could he have let so many years go by? he asked himself wonderingly. She was so beautiful. Why wasn't she his?

He'd spent the night staring at the ceiling and watching the moon make its progress across the sky, puzzling over that very question. His memories of her were treasures, bright and clear and vivid. He'd wanted to see her again. But he'd never expected it to be like this.

She'll be older, he'd thought. Married for eighteen years now, with kids and a husband who will be a nice guy I'll probably like. We'll get together like old friends, talk about old times, laugh a little—and then go our separate ways.

She was older all right, but nothing about her had diminished in any way. She was so much the girl he'd left here years before, and yet at the same time, so different. One look into those green eyes, one feather-light touch of her hand, just the sound of her voice, and he was caught up in it again, as though there had been no time at all between the summer of his eighteenth year and now.

He followed her in through the back door and she turned and looked at him sternly.

"Wait here in the kitchen," she said. "I'll be right back."

As she left the room, he leaned against a counter and looked around. It was a big, warm, welcoming kitchen, with tile counters and wood cabinets and flowers in a vase. There was no evidence of small children, no pictures taped to the refrigerator, no children's toys on the floor.

What was all over the floor were her wet footprints. He amused himself watching them dry until she returned. She'd pulled the band from her braid and let her hair hang free to dry, and she'd also changed into brief yellow shorts and a polka-dot top. His first thought was that he was glad she'd left her brown legs bare. Then he looked into her eyes and saw a cold hostility he hadn't realized she was capable of.

It stunned him. She really didn't want him here. What had happened to change her from the loving girl he'd left behind? There had been no promises, no firm plans. They'd barely known each other for less than a week. What had he done to bring on this resentment?

"I'm sorry," he said. "I know you didn't want me to do this."

She didn't deny his words, moving to the refrigerator and opening the door. "Would you like something to drink?" she asked coolly. "Juice or ice tea?"

"Nothing," he said, shaking his head, then watching as she poured herself some tea and came to the counter to join him.

"Sit down," she said, offering a bar stool while she took one on the other side of the counter. "And tell me when you're leaving."

He wanted to laugh, but he could tell mirth wouldn't be appreciated at this time, so he stifled the impulse. Still, he ignored her question. "You were pretty vehement last night," he said instead.

"I meant every word of it," she replied crisply.

He nodded, studying her. "I know you did. But I meant what I said, too." Reaching across the counter, he took her hand in his. "Don't you remember, Shawnee?" he asked softly, searching her eyes. "Don't you remember how it was?"

She tried to pull her hand away but his grip was too tight and she didn't want to start a struggle, so she left it there.

"That's only one of many memories, Ken," she said shortly. "It's been eighteen years."

He shook his head, wincing. He didn't want to think about her other memories. Of course she was right. It had been a long time and and she'd been so young. Any fool would know she would have had other romances. But he didn't want to think about them, much less hear about them.

"I don't understand you. Why don't you want to remember? What we had was wonderful."

She blinked very quickly and avoided looking him straight in the eye. "It was crazy."

"It was love," he said softly, suddenly realizing that was exactly what it had been. Love. Why hadn't he let himself call it that before? "I was in love. Weren't you?"

Her heart was beating much too fast. She felt as though she were drowning. "Puppy love," she murmured, looking away. "It was only puppy love."

His eyes clouded. "First love," he amended huskily. "It was definitely my first experience with love. And from all the evidence, I'd say that you..."

She couldn't let him go on with this. "Ken, don't you understand—that was so long ago." She stared at him as though the harder she stared, the better the chances of getting through to him. "We have new lives now. You're married and have children..."

He frowned, rearing back. "What are you talking about? I'm not married."

It took a moment for his response to register. "You're...you're not?" She stared at him, thunderstruck, wondering if she could dare believe him.

He shook his head, grimacing. "I've never been married in my life. What gave you the idea that I was married?"

She was bewildered now. He'd cut the legs out from under her. "I—I saw you. There was a blonde in the car...and kids..."

His gaze sharpened. "Where was this? When?"

Her mouth was dry. He wasn't really married. Did this change anything? She wasn't sure. She couldn't think straight. "It doesn't matter."

"Was it before last night?"

She nodded.

Perplexity deepened his voice. "So you knew I was in town and you didn't say anything? Shawnee, what is this? Why are you trying to keep me out of your life this way?" He took her hand in his again, trying to read her expression. "Do you hate me?"

Hate him! That could never, ever be. How could she ever pretend to hate him? But she couldn't speak, couldn't tell him that.

"Do you hate me because of what happened?" he asked softly. "Because we made love? Because we were so young?"

Never. She resented him for many things, but never for helping to conceive Jimmy. Her son was the most wonderful thing in her life. Without him, she would have nothing. But she couldn't tell him that, either.

She looked at him, at the honesty in his face, and the pretense crumbled. "I don't hate you, Ken," she said at last, her eyes full of confusion. "But... you're really not married?"

He shrugged, impatient. Karen and the children really didn't have anything to do with what was going on between the two of them. "Karen is my brother's wife."

"Oh." It was obscene how light her heart felt at the news, as though champagne were sparkling through her veins. She shouldn't be this glad.

"Gary was killed in a car accident in January," he went on, finally recognizing that perhaps a fuller explanation was needed. "Karen hasn't been handling it very well. So I took some time off and brought her and the kids to Hawaii to do some recuperating. They deserve a little happiness. It's been rough on us all, but on Karen the most. Anyway, it gave me a chance to come back and look for you again."

She turned away. She didn't want to talk about the last time he'd come looking for her.

But he wasn't going to leave it alone. "And how about you? When I came through seventeen years ago, I tried to find you. I actually talked to some guy who said he was your brother. He told me about your... your marriage." He paused, but she didn't make a comment. "How did that work out?" he asked softly.

She forced herself to turn and meet his eyes. "I've never been married, either," she told him evenly. "Mack lied. I was out of town visiting relatives. He thought he was protecting me."

"Protecting you?" He rose, anger following confusion across his feature. "What the hell, Shawnee...?"

"He was young." She swallowed hard and shivered, remembering how angry she'd been, how devastated. Her world had seemed to wither away around her. She'd really thought she would never be happy again. "We were all young."

He ran a hand through his hair, ruffling it wildly, trying to stay calm and not succeeding very well. "But I didn't try again because I thought there was no use. All those years..." Another thought occurred to him. "Say, I left him my address so you could write to me. Why didn't you ever write?"

She shook her head. "He tore the address up and threw it away before I ever got back."

He sank back onto his seat, anger mixing with a special brand of horror. It would take time to digest just how big an impact such a simple act had had. "Would you have wanted to see me?" he asked softly, because now, that was really all that mattered. "If you'd known I was looking for you?"

Like nothing else in her life, nothing else in the world. She'd been dying to see him, dying to show him the son they had made together. When she'd found out what Mack had done, she'd gone crazy, destroying her relationship with her brother for years to come. But she couldn't tell him that. There was so much she just couldn't explain to him without giving away her one big secret. She closed her eyes for a moment, then shook her head. "There's no point in going over things we can do nothing about now."

His hands clenched in front of him. That wasn't the answer he'd wanted. "Damn it, Shawnee," he ground out, pinning her with a laserlike glance.

The moment he saw her tragic face, his anger evaporated. He wanted to take her in his arms and hold her. He wanted to make love with her. But most of all, he wanted to blot out the pain in her eyes.

Because it was pain, the emotion he'd seen. The hostility she felt for him was born in pain. But why? What had happened to her since he'd left her that summer day? Somehow he had to find out what had put that anguish there.

"Here I thought I'd find you with a husband and a pack of kids by now," he said gently, touching her arm lightly. "What happened, Shawnee? Why didn't you ever marry?"

She looked up, her eyes flashing. "It wasn't because I was mooning over *you,* Ken Forrest."

He grinned. This was better. She was still prickly, still defensive. But the cold hostility was gone.

"Do you remember when we met?" he asked her.

Did she remember? She'd relived that scene a thousand times in her head. "Yes," she said reluctantly. "I was working in Hiroshi's store that summer."

"And I came to the Big Island with my water polo team to play in a tournament at the high school pool. Our very first game, I took the back of another player's head in my teeth and knocked a couple of them loose."

She smiled. This was irresistible. How many times had she gone over these things by herself, all alone? And now he was willing to go over them with her. There was no way she could fight the temptation to indulge herself in memories. "And got into a fight because of it," she reminded him.

He nodded and his grin was lopsided. "I was a punk, there's no denying it. It wasn't really the kid's fault. It was just part of the play. But I was so full of anger that summer." He shook his head, remembering. "I took it out on him and ended up breaking two fingers on his chin."

"Which took you out of the tournament."

He laughed. "And brought me to Hiroshi's store, looking for aspirin." His smile faded and his eyes softened. "I thought you were a Hawaiian princess when I first saw you."

Her face was dreamy. "And I thought you had the bluest eyes and the widest shoulders I'd ever seen."

"You took me to see that dentist about my teeth."

"My uncle Toki. And you made me laugh all the way home."

"You took me in and fed me dinner. And a bunch of your neighbors and relatives came over and played songs and danced half the night away."

"And you didn't go back to the hotel with the rest of your team that night. You slept on our couch."

Somehow they had gone from holding one hand to holding both and smiling across the counter at one another. They didn't say any more, but they were both thinking about the valley, and the hot summer afternoon when they'd climbed to the waterfall. There would never be a day as crystal clear again. There would never be air as soft or trees as green.

"Do you remember...?" he began, his eyes as deep and blue as the open sea.

"Don't." She closed her eyes for a moment. "Please don't," she whispered.

He frowned, wishing he could make her tell him what the matter was. Her face was so beautiful, her skin so radiant, her eyes so full of emotions. She was everything she had ever been—and more.

"Come with me to Jade Tree Valley," he said at last, knowing they were both thinking the same thing.

Shawnee's eyes widened. Was he nuts? How could she go back there? "No."

"Do you go there often?"

The truth would reveal more than she wanted to let him know, but she told it, anyway. "I've never been back. Not since that day we..." Her voice trailed off, but he knew what she was talking about.

"But you told me it was your favorite place."

She turned so she wouldn't have to look into his eyes. "I was just a kid. Time moves on, you know."

Satisfaction was coursing through him. He knew enough now to know she didn't hate him at all. He still had no idea why she was so defensive, but he could work with it. He wanted only to be with her.

"We should go," he urged. "The two of us."

"No."

He grabbed her hand again. "Come on, Shawnee. It's nothing serious. Go with me. That place has lived in my imagination for so long. I want to go back and see if it lives up to the image I've got of it."

A shadow passed deep in her eyes. "Nothing ever does."

He didn't even have to hesitate. "That's not true. You have."

There was no getting around the fact that it was always nice to hear a compliment. She flushed. She couldn't help it. "You'll have to go alone, Ken," she told him. "I won't go back there."

He knew instinctively that her reluctance to go back had everything to do with the reason she wanted to blot out the past. If he could just get her back there, maybe he could find out what was bothering her. He gazed at her for a long moment, then used a new tact.

"But what am I going to do with my afternoon if you won't come with me?" he asked idly.

She knew he was going to keep at this, and she wasn't sure if she was going to be able to resist. The truth was, she'd dreamed about going back to the valley with him for years. Only, in her dreams, a young boy had gone along with them.

Now the boy wasn't so young any longer. And the dream had faded.

"I'm not an entertainment director," she told him tartly. "You'll have to work out your day's plan for yourself. Sorry."

He shrugged and looked grumpy. "All right, then. I guess I'll have time to go see what Reggie wants."

Fear quivered along her spine. "Reggie? What are you talking about?"

That certainly hit a nerve. He swallowed the self-satisfied grin that threatened. "What is he to you, anyway?" he asked instead of answering. "I know you've never been married to him. Anyone could see through that one. But what is he, an old friend?"

"An old relative is more like it. He's my cousin." She looked at him nervously. "You talked to him last night when I was in the ladies' room, didn't you? What did he say? Did he tell you where I live? Is that how you found me?"

"No. He only told me where *he* lived, and gave me his number." He smiled at her, slowly, sweetly. "I was still in the parking lot, sitting in my car, trying to assimilate seeing you again, when you came out of the restaurant last night. So I followed you home."

She flushed. So he knew she hadn't been able to eat, after all. But there was no use trying to hide the fact that he definitely had a strong effect on her. It stood out like a sore thumb. Still, this reference to seeing Reggie had her worried.

"Reggie said he has a business proposition for me," Ken explained, watching her reaction. "He told me to come around to his place this afternoon if I was interested."

The mermaids again. "Oh, Reggie," she muttered under her breath.

The last thing in the world she wanted was for the two of them to get to be buddies. Reggie was bound to realize who Ken looked like soon enough. And if he let anything slip about Jimmy, Ken would know right away. That couldn't happen. So what was she willing to do to make sure it didn't?

He'd set this thing up from the beginning, and she knew it. Still, if she had to play along to keep her secret under wraps, that was exactly what she would do. But being a good businesswoman, she wanted to get something for her side of the bargain, too.

She gazed at him speculatively. "When are you leaving?"

That surprised him. "Leaving?"

"Going back to the mainland."

"Actually, we've got tickets for Honolulu tomorrow and we leave for California the day after tomorrow. Why?"

She reached out and grabbed his hands with her own. "Do you promise?" she demanded, her eyes full of heartfelt appeal. "Do you promise you'll leave?"

This bewildered him. Why was she so anxious to get rid of him? What didn't she want him to see? Or who didn't she want seeing him? He frowned, looking deep into her eyes.

"Do you really want to get rid of me so badly?" he asked softly.

"I'll go with you to Jade Tree Valley if you promise," she said, ignoring his question. "I'll go with you right now."

His heart was hammering in his chest as he looked deeply into her eyes. Somehow he was bound and determined to unlock the mystery there.

"Okay," he said softly. "I promise."

Four

This was a big mistake. How could she have been so dumb? Anyone with half a brain could have told her not to do this. Going back to the scene of the crime only made things worse. Much, much worse.

"Remember?"

The word was everywhere, echoing in her mind.

It wouldn't have been so bad if the valley had been ruined, if tourists had destroyed it, if plastic wrap and pull tops littered the ground, if teenagers infested the slopes of the mountains. Then she could have said, "Well, isn't that a shame? I guess what they say is true. You can't go back."

But it wasn't that way. The valley was beautiful, lush and green, with birds singing in the trees and a light breeze blowing. There was no one in sight. They had the place to themselves. It was exactly as it had been eighteen years ago.

"Hey." Ken touched her shoulder and she turned to look

at the log he indicated. "Didn't we sit on that? Didn't we rest here?"

She nodded. She remembered every step of that climb.

"Let's sit." He took her hand and tugged her toward the log. "We've got to do everything just like we did it before."

Digging in her heels, she yanked her hand away from him. "Oh, no, we don't," she said sharply. It was best to get that out in the open and settled right away.

"Okay, not everything," he said with a grin. "You call the shots, lady. Your wish will be my command."

She sat, but far enough away from him so that he couldn't casually drape an arm around her shoulders. And then, magically, she was caught up in the spell of the valley again.

"It's so beautiful." She sighed, wanting to reach out and touch the ferns, the trees, the wild orchids that stood out so vividly on the opposite mountainside.

"It is that," he replied quietly, but he wasn't looking at the valley. With his head slightly tilted, he was staring at her, letting his mind go back to how it had been before. She'd worn tight jeans that day, and a pink halter top, and he could remember how her skin seemed to glisten in the sunlight. He'd kissed her while they were sitting right here, his fingers sliding over her, drawing in the heat from her skin, and she'd giggled and told him his touch tickled. He remembered how it had felt, how fire had seemed to sweep through him, heating his blood until he'd thought he couldn't stand it. He'd known they were going to make love. He supposed he should have warned her then, let her have time to make an intelligent choice. But he wasn't intelligent that day. He was young. And very much in love.

"Maybe we should go back," Shawnee said suddenly. She wasn't sure what was going through his mind, but she could sense it was something dangerous. His face was blank, but something in his eyes told her he was remembering things best left lost in the mists of time. "It's a pretty stiff climb after we get around that next bend. Remember?"

His face cleared, back to the present. Cocking an eyebrow, he gave her a questioning look. "Think I can't make it anymore, don't you?" he said, pretending outrage. "You think I'm too old and worn out and out of shape to climb to the waterfall."

She grinned, feeling more comfortable again now that the sultry look had left his face. Reaching back, she began to twist her thick hair into a braid. "Well. Aren't you?"

"Hey, I could climb to that waterfall with you on my back."

"Great. I was hoping for a ride."

He made a pitiful face. "If only I didn't have this recurring back problem," he added quickly. "Then I would be glad to do it. Any time."

"Right." He was just as good at making her laugh now as he had been then. Why did she have to like him so much?

"In the meantime," he suggested, leaning back, enjoying watching her fix her hair, "we should just sit here and talk, don't you think? Just to make sure we store up enough energy."

She shook her head in mock scorn. "Let me know when you're rested enough, grandpa," she said. "Too bad I didn't bring my knitting." Hair secured, she asked, "So... what shall we talk about?"

"You."

That topic wasn't safe. She glanced at him and shook her head. "No. Let's talk about you."

He grimaced. "There's nothing to talk about there."

Turning on the log, she brought up one leg and leaned back so that she could look at him. He looked even younger in the open sunlight, his hair suddenly blonder, his eyes as blue as the sky behind him. His skin wasn't very tanned, but it was smooth and firm, and that square jaw still looked as rock-hard as ever. He'd ruined her for other men, she suddenly realized. He'd come and gone, and no man she'd ever met had measured up. Damn you, Ken Forrest, she thought silently as she stared at him. Damn you for making me set my standards too high.

"There's plenty to talk about regarding you," she retorted out loud, head to the side as she studied him. "For instance, tell me why you never got married."

He closed his eyes, head tilted to catch the sun. "It just never really came up."

"I don't believe that. After all this time?" She poked his leg with the toe of her shoe. "Tell me."

Opening one eye, he glared at her. "There's nothing to tell."

She sighed. "Okay, let's do this another way. What happened after you left here that summer?"

"I went to college."

"And never had a date the whole four years?"

He opened both eyes this time, but mainly to zero in on a fly he wanted to swat. "Oh, I dated, all right. You want to hear about that sort of thing?"

What did he think she was interested in, his wardrobe? "I want to hear all about it."

He sat up a little straighter and gave the impression of thinking hard about the topic. "Okay. Yeah, I dated. I did the usual things. Fraternity parties, ski trips, weekends at the beach. Nothing special. Nothing lasting."

She loved hearing that, but she knew she was living in a dreamworld if she actually believed it.

"And then?" she prodded.

"I went to law school. Didn't have time to eat and sleep, much less have a relationship. And when that was over, I toured Europe."

Okay. There had to be a story there. After all, he had to admit he had a history of romance while on holiday. "And I suppose you fell in love with an Italian countess,'' she suggested, hoping against hope that it wasn't true.

"Hardly. Nothing that exotic. When you're touring Europe with a pack on your back, staying in student hostels, you don't mix with the royalty much. I wouldn't say romance was a main event in my life during that time." He chuckled, remembering. "But, of course, there was Betty Jo the Hobo."

She frowned. That didn't sound right. "Betty Jo the Hobo?''

He grinned, pleased to have ruffled her complacency. "Yup. Colorful character. She and I hitchhiked across the Continent together for almost six months. I guess you could call that a relationship of sorts."

Six months. That was certainly a lot longer than she'd had him for. She wished now she'd never brought this subject up. But since it was sitting there, right in front of them, she had to know the rest. "Were you in love with her?" she asked in a small voice, trying to look completely disinterested.

"With Betty Jo?" He laughed aloud. "Not quite. She wasn't into commitment in those days. She'd sleep with anyone who would give us directions. She wasn't really my type." He sobered, thinking back. "No, we were more like pals. We just hung out together because we were going to the same places. I heard from her the other day. She runs a jazz club in Fort Lauderdale now."

They were both silent for a moment, then he slid off the log and reached out to help her down. "We might as well get going," he said. "We've got a waterfall to meet up with."

They started along the trail, but Shawnee couldn't get the hitchhiking woman out of her mind. "That Betty Jo person?" she began as they climbed.

"Yeah?" he responded, looking surprised, his mind obviously on to new things.

"She was in love with you, wasn't she?"

He stopped and looked at her quizzically. "How did you know that?"

"Woman's intuition." She passed him on the trail, not stopping.

"Oh, woman's intuition," he mocked right back at her, catching up with ease. "That enduring myth."

"It's not a myth at all. It's very real." She gazed at him steadily as they walked side by side. "Women know things men don't."

Humor danced in his eyes. "Sure. And they're closer to Mother Earth, aren't they?"

"Maybe."

"Well, let women have intuition, if that's what they want. Men have basic instinct."

They both halted as they came to the top of a rise and looked down at a small raging torrent of water at their feet. The little river was racing downhill and there wasn't a way to cross it in sight. Obviously, no one had come this way for a long time.

"How convenient," Shawnee said wryly. "What does your basic instinct tell you about how we're going to get across this stream?"

It took more than instinct, or even intuition. It took imagination and ingenuity, but together they rigged up a bridge of sorts out of fallen branches propped against conveniently placed rocks. Working quickly, they made it without getting too wet, holding hands as they crossed. And once on the other side, they resumed their conversation.

"Tell me more about your girlfriends," Shawnee urged. She wanted to hear everything. She wasn't sure what she hoped to gain from hearing all this, but she knew it had something to do with justifying what had happened, validating the past. "What happened after Europe?"

"I passed the bar and started working, and from then on, it's been a roller-coaster ride. I've been working too hard ever since to even think about dating."

She swatted at a mosquito. "Oh, come on. I don't really believe that."

He turned and looked at her, half teasing. "It's true. I'm just a quiet guy. Not for me the social whirl."

She threw him a challenging look over her shoulder. "Ken Forrest, are you trying to tell me you haven't had a date in ten years?"

He hesitated. "Well, not exactly."

"Aha."

She was cute, sending him those looks, her eyes so bright. He grinned, coming up beside her. "Okay, you got me. I've been out with women now and then, but nothing serious. Some of it was fun, some regrettable."

He thought for a moment about Sheila, the secretary the firm had first assigned him. She had chased him for months until he finally bedded her on the couch in his office. That was one he wasn't too proud of, and he certainly wasn't going to tell Shawnee about it. He glanced at her sideways.

"Anyway, we've been talking a lot about me. Now what about you?"

"Me?" She shook her head dismissively. "I've hardly looked at another man since that summer."

Turning, he grabbed her around the waist and laughed down into her face. "I knew it. You've been carrying the torch all these years, haven't you?"

She flushed and pushed him away, wishing it didn't make her tingle all over just to touch him. "Ken Forrest, where did you get such a big ego?" she murmured, moving along the path with renewed energy.

"What else am I to make of this?" His tone was almost sly. "You certainly fell for me quickly enough."

She whirled, outrage in her eyes. "Oh, right," she said, sarcasm dripping from her words. "Head over heels. It was love at first sight."

He shrugged, sobering, searching her eyes. "That was certainly what it felt like," he said softly.

She turned away, biting her lip, wishing they hadn't gone down this route. "The truth is," she tried rather feebly, "it was such a shock dealing with you, it's taken me years to get over it and trust men once more."

He stopped her again, grabbing her wrists and pulling her around to face him. "Tell me the truth, Shawnee," he said, his gaze caressing her face. "Did it feel like love to you? Weren't we in love back then? Or was I dreaming?"

She didn't want this. This was much too dangerous. It brought back more than memories. It brought back feelings.

She'd been so young, so vulnerable. With her father dead and her mother gone most of the time, looking for work, she'd been overwhelmed, trying to do what she could to raise her three younger brothers. Talk about growing up too fast. As she looked back now, she could understand how she had succumbed to the temptation Ken had brought into her life. She just wanted to make sure it didn't happen again.

"We barely knew each other," she said, using the same defense she'd used before and feeling less and less sure of it. "It felt like love, but..."

"If it wasn't love, you wouldn't have brought me up here that day," he said, his intense gaze daring her to contradict him.

He was right, and she knew it. Jade Tree Valley, her enchanted, magic world, her private place since childhood. She'd brought him here as a gift of love. And he'd given her Jimmy in return.

"Maybe it was love," she whispered, "but..."

He kissed her. Softly, gently, as lightly as morning dew, his lips touched hers and then they were gone again.

"It was love," he said decisively. "You can't take that away from me."

He was off again, climbing the path, and she was following, her heart beating more from his kiss than from the effort to keep up with him. She was totally confused. Did he really look back on the time they'd had together as the one love of his life? Were they really that much alike? It wasn't possible. That would be too good to be true.

She caught up with him at the bend in the trail. He'd stopped and was leaning against a tree, waiting for her.

"Want to rest?" he asked, and she nodded.

They sank down and let the breeze cool their skin.

"Finish your story," she said, watching him under lowered lashes. "You haven't told me everything."

He looked back steadily. "I have no more story."

"I don't believe that." The corners of her mouth tilted. "Tell me about the woman you almost married."

His face registered surprise. She'd done it again. That damn intuition. "How did you know there was a woman I almost married?"

How did she know? Puh-leese! But Shawnee grinned. "There's always one of those. Come on. Give."

He thought for a moment, a bemused smile on his face, studying her and the way the sunlight cast shadows that only made her more beautiful.

"Okay," he said at last. "There was someone. Kathleen Sessions was her name. She was tall, beautiful, very elegant, and a fellow lawyer. We worked together on a couple of cases, and that worked out so well, I thought, why not go ahead and make it permanent? After all, I was about thirty then. I figured it was time to get married. So we got engaged."

Shawnee forced herself to keep a light tone. It was absolutely humiliating how his words cut into her like knives. It wasn't supposed to be this way. She wasn't supposed to care. "You haven't said anything about loving her."

Turning, he looked into her eyes, his own so utterly honest, she almost flinched, as though looking into the sun. "Love didn't have anything to do with it," he said slowly. "Honest, it didn't."

Her heart leapt again, and she wished that it wouldn't. "What happened?" she asked, quickly averting her eyes, afraid of letting him see too much.

"We went along okay for a while. But then I began to realize there was something missing."

"What could be missing? If she was beautiful, intelligent..." If she went on with this, she would choke.

But he didn't notice. He hesitated, trying to put his feelings into words. "There was a warmth missing. A depth of feeling. I'd seen it before, felt it before. I knew it was possible. But it wasn't there."

She didn't want to ask the obvious question, but she felt a glow building in her chest—a very dangerous glow, and she wished she could somehow put it out.

"We'd better get going," she said, rising and dusting off her bottom. "We're taking twice as long to get there as we did last time."

"We're savoring the moment," he replied, but he rose and joined her. They were almost to their destination, and he was looking forward to it.

They went on for a few minutes, clamoring over rocks, pushing aside greenery. And then came the moment they'd both been waiting for.

"Can you hear it?" Ken reached out and helped her across a tiny stream.

She didn't answer, but she smiled at him, feeling the same excitement she could see in his eyes. The waterfall. The rush of the water thundered ahead. She could already feel a mist in the air.

They climbed steadily now and neither of them said anything else until they'd reached the crest of the rise and stood side by side.

He took her hand and they stood together, gazing at the awesome cascades, marveling as the diamond beads of water shot over the cliff and fell in a stunning necklace around the mountain's throat. The power of it seemed to fill the air around them. They stood very still, letting the sound wash over them, feeling the spray on their faces. And finally Ken turned to her.

"Coming in?" he asked, beginning to unbutton his shirt.

It was as much a challenge as an invitation, and her returning smile held the same defiance.

"Sure," she said, and reached to pull her top over her head.

She knew he was remembering the time before, when they'd both shucked off every stitch of clothing and gone swimming together in the nude. The look on his face when he saw that she'd worn a swimsuit underneath this time was comical, and she laughed out loud.

"I'm older now," she teased him. "Older and wiser, and I come prepared."

"You know what?" He yanked open his zipper and let his slacks fall to the ground, revealing his own swimming trunks. "So do I."

She met his gaze and they both burst into laughter. A feeling of connection was growing between them, something above and beyond the physical pull they were both fighting so hard. It was nice to feel like she had a real friend in him. But as their laughter faded and her gaze fell to his bared chest, she felt her stomach contract and the quiver start deep inside once again.

He'd been a strong, muscular boy, but this...this was the chest of a man with defined muscles and a light coating of golden hair, and one glance burned the sight of it into her mind for all time. She looked away quickly, but she knew she would never lose that image.

"Last one in is a rotten egg," he called, dropping his shirt and turning toward the pond at the base of the waterfall.

She peeled away her shorts and ran to follow him into the water, needing the coolness to calm down the flames threatening to burn inside her. It was wonderful, fresh and light, like swimming in champagne. They laughed and played together like a pair of dolphins for a half hour, then they pulled themselves up onto the bank and sat back to dry off.

"Thanks for coming with me, Shawnee," he told her, stretching back and looking into the water. "This has been great. Just like I remembered it."

She nodded, her smile bemused, but her mind was on another day, another time. They'd cavorted in the water much the same way, but they had been so young, they hadn't known how to control the way their bodies seemed to need each other. Every touch was like another bit of fuel for the fire. At first they'd pretended to ignore each other's nakedness, but that didn't last for long. Soon he was cupping her breast as she floated past, and she was letting her fingers trail across his flat belly when she splashed him, and then they were kissing and his hand was reaching between her legs....

She gasped softly, closing her eyes, trying to savor that feeling and reject it at the same time.

Ken stared at her as though he could read her mind. The need to reach for her was growing inside him like a monster, something he knew was going to be hard to overcome. He wished she were wearing the electric blue suit, but she'd changed into a two-piece of a much more sensible cut and a much less transparent fabric. Still, he hardly saw her as she looked now. He didn't have to close his eyes to see her as she had been that day once they'd come out of the water and flopped down on the banks. They had been sitting in almost the same place they were now. Everything about her had filled him with an incredible joy and an overwhelming need of possession. Her long legs, her neatly cut navel, the line of her hips, everything called to him. Her rounded breasts had gleamed in the sun, and he'd started off licking water from them as a joke, but the joke had quickly been forgotten and his movements had slowed, slowly savoring every drop. She'd sighed and sunk her fingers into his thick hair, writhing with feelings so new to her, she'd been trembling with fear as well as anticipation. He'd fumbled, not really sure of what he was doing, but very sure he was going to do it. And she'd leaned back... here....

He reached out and put the flat of his hand down where she'd been, where he'd felt her lift her hips to welcome him, where he'd plunged inside her, giving release to feelings that had been much too strong to resist.

He'd hardly had time to revel in the sensation because he'd been afraid that he'd hurt her, so he'd come away quickly. They'd lain together, side by side, right on this spot, and he'd held her in his arms and rocked her and whispered things into her ear, and then she'd been ready to try again. He took it slower the second time, more concerned with her than with his own needs. And when she finally caught the wave and cried out and dug her fingers into his back, he found out what it meant to find real fulfillment.

Right here. He flattened his hand on the spot and turned to look at Shawnee, his current need almost as fierce as the one he'd felt that day.

"No." She saw the glazed look in his eyes and her heart jumped, instinctively knowing what he was thinking. "No, Ken." She began to back away, shaking her head.

Turning from her, he closed his eyes, swore harshly, then rose and dove into the water and swam for the other side. She was absolutely right. They weren't playing that game. That wasn't what they were here for. They weren't going to do that again. They weren't in love this time.

She watched him swim away and wanted to cry, then hated herself for that weakness. What would she cry for? Days gone by? Or wanting him now and not letting herself have him?

He was just a tourist. He would be leaving soon. He'd been young before, and so had she. She was older now. She was supposed to be wiser. Wasn't she?

Yes. She was much, much wiser. And she was going to be proud of herself in the morning this time.

When he pulled himself back out of the water, he turned and smiled at her, and she could see in his eyes that he'd come to terms with how things had to be. His smile was open and friendly. He knew they didn't have to recreate the entire scene to enjoy this.

She felt relief spilling through her and it wasn't until then that she realized how hard this had been on both of them. For years she'd had nothing but her son and her memories to remind her of Ken. Now those memories were going to be enhanced by this visit. She felt as though she were suddenly a richer woman for it.

The trip back down was twice as fast as the climb up had been. They jogged along together, sometimes holding hands, laughing, pointing out things along the way. He drew her close to show her a purple lizard, curling her into the crook of his arm, and she felt a burst of affection toward him. In some ways, they were closer now than they'd ever been.

Her heart was light and every step she took was full of joy. She was in her beloved valley with the only man she'd ever loved, the father of her son. She'd found out something very important to her—it had been right to love him. He was special, it hadn't just been an immature crush. He was a great guy.

Would he have been a great father? She would never know that. When he'd first reentered her life the day before she'd been sure he wouldn't be. She'd tried to tell herself for years now that it was just as well he'd been out of Jimmy's life. Now, she had to admit, she wasn't so sure. He was everything she remembered and more. She loved being with him.

But that didn't mean he would have stood the test of fatherhood. From what she'd experienced, most men seemed to shy away from it if they had the chance. It was just as well, she kept telling herself. It was just as well.

The one thing she had to regret was that Jimmy had never known him. She could see now that he would have been a good role model in a lot of ways. Jimmy had done very well with the uncles and cousins he'd grown up with. But a little of Ken couldn't have hurt him. She knew every boy did better with a father around.

Okay, she had to admit it to herself, at least, Ken would have been a good father. It was a shame he hadn't had that chance. Now, it was too late.

But pushing the parental issue aside, Ken was a terrific guy to be with, better than any other man she had ever known. If only this trip could last forever.

But she knew it was almost over. She'd gone to the valley with him and he'd promised to leave if she did. By this time tomorrow, he would be gone. And suddenly she knew it was going to hurt again. It was going to hurt a lot.

But he has to go, she reminded herself urgently. The sooner the better.

Ken's feelings were less ambiguous. He wanted to stay. He hadn't felt so alive in years. He felt as though he were breathing again, as though he'd been in a coma for a very long time and had finally come out of it. He wanted to pick Shawnee up and whirl her around, like they did in those dopey movies. Now that he'd seen her again, he knew that the memories staying with him the way they had was no fluke. There was something, a special tie that bound the two of them together and always would, and he knew she could feel it, too. Why she wanted him to get lost so quickly, he couldn't guess. He wasn't going to be here for long, anyway. Why not take advantage of the time they did have?

He was going to have to talk to her about that, but he'd wait until they were back at her house. He was a lawyer, for God's sake. Surely he could think of some way to talk her into letting him stay.

Suddenly he found himself whistling. Whistling! He hadn't done that since he was a kid. He felt great, better than when he won a difficult case.

Hey, it was almost like being in love.

Five

Ken's rental car was right where they'd left it. He glanced at the time, had one brief pang of contrition that he'd left Karen and the kids alone for so long, then looked at the woman next to him in the passenger seat and forgot all about that. He wanted to be with her. Hell, he needed to be with her. There *had* to be some way to talk her into letting him off the hook on his promise.

"That was fun," he said casually. "How about we do it again in another eighteen years?"

She laughed, stretching back, feeling so comfortable with him. "It's a deal," she said, then watched as he backed the car out of the parking area and headed for the highway.

He was good to look at, very like Jimmy, and yet very different. Jimmy had her family's build, rounder, a little thicker. But his eyes and mouth were so very much the same. She was being pricked by a few guilty pangs. The old arguments resurfaced. Didn't Ken have a right to know about his son?

No, she told herself. He had no such rights. Eighteen years of absence had taken those rights from him. Jimmy had a settled idea of what had happened to his father. All finding out about Ken could do was tear that apart. It would destroy everything she'd built their lives on.

A part of her reluctance to let him in was pure selfishness, and she knew it. Jimmy was all she had in the world. She'd been both father and mother to him all this time. She didn't want to share him with someone who was bound to change things, someone who would turn their world upside down. She couldn't bear the thought of it.

She was fighting hard for Jimmy's soul right now as it was, fighting the wild kids he sometimes hung out with, fighting that girlfriend, Misty. She didn't need another adversary in the struggle.

"I'm going to have to stop for gas," he said, pulling into Chang's little three-pump station on the corner.

They were still a few miles from where she lived, but she was known here. Quietly, she slid down lower in the seat and picked up a road map, studying it closely in an effort to cover her face, while Ken got out and started pumping. A man in greasy overalls came out to talk to him and she relaxed a little. It was no one she knew.

Ken was finishing up when she heard the familiar roar of a VW bug engine. Her heart stood still, and she held her breath, not daring to look around the map.

There was the clanking sound of a car door opening. "Hey, Hondo." The voice left no room for doubt. It was her son Jimmy. "Are you going to be home later tonight? I've got to..."

The voice faded as Jimmy disappeared into the mechanics' area. Hondo was a friend of his who worked here part-time, one of the ones she wasn't crazy about. But that didn't concern her right now. All she cared about was getting Ken out of here before he saw Jimmy.

Ken was opening the car door. Thank God. She glanced back at the garage and saw Jimmy starting to come back out toward his car. Her heart skipped a beat.

"Let's go," she urged, her voice higher than usual. "It's time we got back."

Ken nodded. "Just a minute. I'm waiting for my change." And he turned toward the little office where the attendant had gone with his bill.

Shawnee held her breath, dread sending adrenaline pumping through her body. They were going to walk right past each other. She didn't bother to put the map back up. It was all over, anyway.

Closer and closer they came, and it looked to her as though they were moving in slow motion. She waited for their eyes to meet, waited for disaster. But Jimmy was talking to the skinny youth walking alongside him, and Ken was intent on finding that attendant with his change. Neither one of them glanced at the other, and Jimmy didn't look her way, either. In another moment he was in his car and roaring out onto the highway again, headed away from home.

She let her breath out in a painful rush and collapsed back against the seat, heart thumping. That had been much too close. A good shake-up like that brought reality back into focus. She had to get Ken out of here.

She had trouble composing herself before Ken returned to the car, but she managed. They drove the rest of the way home in silence. Ken could feel the new mood in the car right away, but he didn't understand it.

"How about going for a drink somewhere?" he suggested as her driveway came into view. "A cup of coffee, maybe?"

She shook her head. The joy had gone out of the day, and there wasn't much time. She had no idea where Jimmy had gone or when he would be back. "I'm sorry, Ken," she said briskly, "I've got things I have to do."

He pulled his car up to her house, shut off the engine, and turned to look at her. "What's the matter, Shawnee?" he asked quietly. "What happened?"

"Nothing. I-it's just later than I thought."

He frowned, at a loss. The hostility had returned to her eyes and the mood between the two of them had gone back to being awkward. The acrid taste of frustration welled up in his throat and he wanted to shake her. "Damn it, Shawnee," he said, his voice low and angry. "How can I fix this if you won't tell me what it is?"

As if he could fix everything, kiss it and make it well. She turned away, reaching for the door handle. "I've got to get going," she muttered as she rose from her seat.

He came out of his side of the car and closed the door. "Mind if I come in, too?" he asked coolly.

"Ken, I . . ."

"Just for a drink of water," he said, his gaze level. "Surely you can't deny your climbing partner a drink of water?"

She gave up, turning toward the house. "All right," she said crisply. "But just one drink, and then you're off."

He took long enough about it, slowly sipping the tall, cool glass of water as he leaned against her kitchen counter and watched her above the rim. She made a show of getting things out for dinner preparations and avoided meeting his gaze. Inside, she was counting the seconds and mentally urging him to hurry up and get going. What was he going to do, drink the place dry? For a moment, she considered offering him a thermos to take along, but then she decided against arousing suspicion by being too anxious.

Ken used the time to go over different theories in his mind as to why she was acting like this. He had a feeling if he just thought long and hard enough, he should be able to figure it out. That was the way he lived his life. If circumstances presented you with problems, you found a way to solve them.

A sound out in the driveway brought both their heads around, but it was only a scuffle between two mynah birds and Ken looked back in time to see the start of fear that was just fading from her face. She'd been afraid, just then. Afraid of what? Of someone else arriving? She'd turned back to the counter and was peeling carrots, but her shoulders were hunched stiffly.

He frowned, baffled. Fear. That was what it was. She was horribly afraid of something. What the hell could it be? It wasn't him. She'd been fine when they were alone together in the valley. It had to be fear of someone else. But who? He had an urge to take her in his arms and hold her and find out what she was so afraid of.

He came across the room, put down his glass, then touched her shoulder, but when she turned and looked up into his eyes, her own were bland and emotionless, and he had to wonder if he was imagining things.

"Are you finished with that water?" she asked pointedly.

His smile was just as bland as hers. "Not quite," he said, knowing this was driving her crazy. "I need a refill." And he reached around her to fill his glass at the tap.

Shawnee was on pins and needles. She wanted so badly to get him out of here before Jimmy got back, and he didn't seem to want to budge an inch. What was she going to have to do, throw him bodily out the door?

"You're leaving the island tomorrow, right?" she said firmly, automatically putting her carrots all in a long, neat row without thinking about how odd that looked.

He frowned at the carrots, but when he looked back at her, his eyes clouded. "I don't get it, Shawnee," he said.

She pulled out a bunch of celery and began to yank the stalks apart. "What don't you get?" she said, like a busy woman being interrupted by an annoying child.

"Why are you so anxious to get rid of me? What's happening that you want me out of the way for?"

Oh, why couldn't he just leave? "I've told you before," she said with patient deliberation. "I've got a life here and I don't want to disrupt it."

"How am I disrupting your life?"

She looked up at him, exasperated. "Oh, Ken, be serious. You disrupt my life every time you show up."

"But I don't show up that often." He touched her cheek with the back of his index finger. "Now that I've found you again, Shawnee, I really don't want to let you go so quickly."

Her heart lurched, but she hid it well. Setting her mouth primly, she whacked off the ends of the celery stalks and set them in an orderly line beside the carrots. "A promise is a promise. You can't go back on your word."

He stared at her for a moment, then turned as though to go. "I told you I'd go, and I'll go. But I'll make you another promise, Shawnee. I'm coming back."

She dropped the knife and whirled, staring after him. This was just what she'd known would happen. Finding Ken again had opened Pandora's box. Now she would never be able to rest easy again. Without thinking, she followed him to the door. "When?" she asked breathlessly.

"Maybe next summer. Maybe sooner."

By next summer Jimmy would be starting at the university, unless something went wrong between now and then. She would be in a better position by then, and she would deal with the threat from Ken as she had to.

"Great," she said, trying for a flip tone. "We'll see you then." She gave him a little shove toward the door.

He turned and caught her hand, suddenly sure he knew what it was. "It's another man, isn't it?" he demanded, and something sharp twisted in his gut. "Why can't you just come out and tell me, Shawnee? I can understand a thing like that." Not like it, but understand it. "It stands to reason that a woman like you would have a man around somewhere."

It was almost funny, but she didn't feel much like laughing. His eyes were burning as he looked down at her, and she felt something inside respond, reach out, crave connection. But she couldn't give in to those feelings, not if she was going to save anything from this wreck of a day.

"Just go, Ken. Please."

"*Is* it another man?"

"No." She pushed her hair back impatiently. "There is no man in my life. I swear to you. Now will you go?"

He didn't believe her. How could he? If it wasn't another man—someone she was afraid would see him here and be angry—what on earth was it? He stared at her for another long moment, but no answers appeared in her face, and he had to give it up. He held her with one long, last look full of bewildered anger, then turned and went down the stairs quickly, striding to his car. She watched him go, her fist balled against her mouth. She was losing him again. And this time she was doing it to herself.

He got into the car and turned to begin backing out. Just before he got to the end of the driveway, a beat-up VW bug roared in, braking hard to avoid hitting him.

Shawnee gasped. "No," she cried, but it was a whisper against her hand. There was nothing she could do now.

The two of them looked each other over, the man and the boy. Ken rolled down his window and said something to Jimmy. She could see Jimmy shaking his head, then the two of them stared at each other. Suddenly Jimmy stepped on the accelerator again and stormed into his usual parking place. Instead of going on out the driveway, Ken directed his car back to the house. He got out slowly, staring at Jimmy who was already out and leaning against his VW.

They were talking to each other, but she couldn't hear what they were saying, and she couldn't stand not knowing. She reached for the door, her fingers trembling, and went out onto the porch.

They both looked up at her, the one with all the answers, and she stood very still, wishing this were all a bad dream, praying she would wake up soon. But she knew that was useless. She was going to have to open up the past to them both, these two who meant so much to her, these two who were the most affected by what had happened, what she'd done. As she stared at them, she suddenly realized the three of them were all links in a common chain. Each one represented a bond with the other two.

Jimmy was walking toward her. His green eyes were wide with shock. Stopping at the bottom of the steps, he pointed at Ken. "Mom? Who is this guy?" he asked her, his voice strained.

She stood very straight and tall, her chin jutting out. She had to stand that way or she would crumple like a pile of old rags on the stairs. "He's an old friend."

Jimmy turned and stared at Ken, and she finally allowed herself to look at him. He was standing in the middle of the driveway, evidently speechless, his face ashen, his gaze riveted on Jimmy.

"Why is he looking at me like that?" Jimmy asked, and suddenly his voice sounded very young, as it had sounded when he was just beginning to turn into a teenager. "What's the matter with him?"

Her mouth was so dry, she couldn't move her lips quickly enough to answer him before Ken stepped closer, grabbed him by the shirt, and demanded, "How old are you?"

Jimmy seemed caught up in the intensity of Ken's gaze. The veins were standing out in Ken's arms, and the throbbing at his temple was visible from where Shawnee stood. Jimmy stared back at him and didn't try to pull away, almost as though he were fascinated, like a cobra to a flute. "I'm seventeen," he said, looking apprehensive.

Ken looked as though someone had hit him, hard, and when he spoke, his voice was ragged and broken, like shards of glass. "Born when? April? May?"

Jimmy tried to pull away, frowning. "May third. Why?"

Ken closed his eyes, but his lips were moving, almost as though he were praying, and his fingers were still clenching Jimmy's shirt.

Shawnee couldn't move. She stood as though paralyzed, as though, if she didn't move, it would all fade away and turn out to be a bad dream.

But Ken was saying something. He had let go of Jimmy and he was coming up the stairs toward her.

"How could you do this to me?" he was saying, or maybe just his eyes were saying it, maybe he hadn't said the words out loud, but it was there, the accusation, the bewildered resentment, and she had to stand firm and glare right back into the outrage of his face.

"I didn't do anything to you," she said. "You have very little to do with this."

"Very little to do..." He turned and looked down at Jimmy again. "Look at him. It's written all over him. My God, Shawnee, how could you keep this from me?"

Jimmy knew. He had to know. But he was still in denial. "What's he talking about, Mom?" he said harshly, his face dark with foreboding. "Tell me what he means."

She looked from one to the other and her heart was breaking. She'd hurt them both and she'd never wanted to hurt either. They were the two people she'd loved more than any other people on earth. It was agony to her, but she couldn't let them know. She had to keep control of the situation or it would fly off into a million pieces and there was no telling what would happen then.

Forcing herself to turn regally, she said, "Come in the house and sit down and we'll talk about it," and then she went on in. They followed her, Jimmy eyeing Ken suspiciously, Ken looking at Jimmy in wonder. She led them into the living room and sat on the couch, sitting back as though she were at ease, when what she really wanted to do was curl into a ball and close her eyes and blot this all out forever.

Jimmy sank onto the edge of the seat next to her. "What's going on, Mom?" he said again, his green eyes clouded with anger, begging her to tell him what he was thinking wasn't really true.

Looking into those eyes, she knew things would never be quite the same between the two of them again. But she would have time to mourn that later. Right now, she had to tell the truth and hope he would understand. She had to be strong. If she didn't do this, the story would get all twisted and ruined. She had to tell it her way. Jimmy had to understand.

"You've always known that I wasn't married to your father," she started out, clasping her hands together in her lap, mostly to control the trembling that threatened to break out. The only thing betraying the upheaval in her soul were her very white knuckles.

Jimmy shrugged impatiently, too busy searching her face to notice the knuckles. "Sure."

She took a quick extra breath. "I explained to you how it happened—"

"Yeah, yeah," he interjected as though he'd heard it all before a hundred times. "You were too young to fall in love but you did, anyway. And he left to go back to the mainland, but his plane crashed and that was the end of that." He moved as though he were suddenly uncomfortable with his body. "That was what you said. That was what everyone always told me."

"That was what I said," she agreed. "That was what I told everyone." She glanced at Ken quickly. He hadn't moved. "Well, everything was true except that last part."

Jimmy sat very still, his face impassive, his eyes hardening into ice. "He didn't die in a plane crash," he said in an emotionless monotone.

She nodded, wishing he were still a little boy and she could pull him into her lap and hold him tight and keep all nightmares at bay. "That's right."

Jimmy didn't turn his head, but he looked sideways at Ken. "Is that him?" he asked, his voice as cool as though he were asking what they were having for dinner.

There was a lump in Shawnee's throat, but she forced it back and managed to whisper, "Yes."

Jimmy turned and looked at him fully, but he continued to talk exclusively to his mother. "Where did he come from all of a sudden?"

Tears were burning in her eyes but she clenched her jaw very hard and held them back. She had to make sure he understood. "Jimmy... he never knew about you."

Jimmy looked back at her, his eyes glacial. "No? Why not?"

She glanced at Ken. His face was stricken, but his eyes looked deep and black, as though he were taking all this in and trying to get clear on what it all meant. "I—I was never able to get in touch with him."

Jimmy gave a dismissive shrug with only one shoulder. "Why didn't he get in touch with you?"

She leaned forward, desperate that he not hold this against Ken. "He tried. He really did. Things just didn't work out."

Jimmy turned slowly and looked at Ken, then straightened and looked back at her. "For seventeen years, my dad's been dead," he said slowly. "Now all of a sudden he's alive." He turned to stare into Ken's eyes. "So what?" he said coldly. "I've done okay without him all this time, I guess it's a little late to get all sentimental over it, don't you think?" He rose from his seat, checked his back pocket for his wallet, and looked very much as though he were about to go out the door and disappear into the night. "Listen, it's been nice meeting you. Hope you have a nice trip back to wherever you came from." He turned as if to go.

Shawnee jumped up and stopped him with a hand on his arm. "Jimmy, he didn't know. How could he do anything if he didn't know about it?"

Jimmy stared back at her. He was no longer her little boy. He was something remote and unsympathetic. He didn't like her right now. He didn't like anybody right now. "He should have known," he said with simple logic. "But it doesn't matter now. I'm all grown up. I don't need a daddy anymore."

He said the word—daddy—with scorn, as though it were something he'd never wanted, something he couldn't imagine needing. She knew he was hurting inside, but what she didn't know was how to help him, how to reach in and soothe him with just the right words, just the right moves. Still, she did know he should stay and get to know the man who was his father.

"Don't go, Jimmy," she said. "Please stay and talk with us."

"'Us'?" He pulled away from her hold on his arm. "You two are an 'us'?"

For just a moment she could see the utter panic in his eyes, and then a wall came down with a thud and all she saw was ice.

"Jimmy, it's not like that," she told him earnestly. "Come back and sit down and get to know Ken." Knowing her son, she tried a challenge. "You can't dislike him until you know him. It doesn't work that way."

"I don't need to know him."

"Yes, you do. It isn't fair to dismiss him without giving him a chance. You're not like that. I know you."

He hesitated, looking back at the new man in his life, and Shawnee knew she almost had him. But just before relief swept in, a set of delicate little knuckles rapped on the still open front door.

"Jimmy?" It was Misty, dressed to kill and pouting prettily. "I waited by the corner, but when you didn't show up..." Moussed hair fell over one eye and her lips were painted magenta. The jersey top was tight and low-cut, and there very obviously was no bra. Misty had an extensive arsenal and she knew how to use it.

Jimmy threw Shawnee a defiant look and strode quickly toward the door. "Sorry, Mother," he said briskly, using the formal address he never used with her. "Got a date. I'll see you later." And he was gone.

Shawnee stood staring after them, stunned and not reacting with her usual deftness. He'd escaped. But wait. He'd gone off full of anger and pain and that was no good. Uttering a little cry, she started for the door, only to find Ken suddenly blocking her path.

"Let me go," she said fretfully, trying to push past him, not thinking rationally, just reacting with pure emotion.

He held her shoulders in his large hands and didn't budge an inch. "Where?" he demanded. "What do you think you're going to do?"

She focused her gaze on him as though she'd suddenly realized who he was. "Jimmy. I want to go after him."

He didn't release her. Slowly he shook his head. "You can't go after him."

Look who was giving orders. She tried and failed to twist out of his hold on her. "Why not?" she cried. "He's my son."

He stared at her. They were talking about his son, too. This was a concept that was going to take a long, long time to get used to. Something stirred deep inside him and he wasn't sure if it was revulsion or exhilaration. He needed some time to absorb this. And he was sure Jimmy needed the same thing.

"I think you ought to let him be alone to think things over."

And who had asked what he thought? "What if he shouldn't be alone?" She thought of Misty in her tight, short skirt, and shuddered. "What if he does something crazy?"

Slowly he shook his head. "He won't do anything crazy. I don't think so."

She searched his eyes, looking for reassurance but not sure he was capable of giving it to her. "How do you know? You don't really know him."

His eyes clouded. "No. I don't know him." He hesitated, then added softly, "But I know there's a part of me in him."

The fight drained out of her and as she let her shoulders sag, he let her go. She turned and stumbled back into the room, then looked at him, slightly bewildered. Leaning against the back of a chair, she slowly regained her strength, watching him saunter back into the room, look about himself with new appreciation. He went from bookcase to bookcase, handling her things, her carved ivory ball, her collection of netsuke figures, her Samoan war club, looking at her books, her set of Shakespeare, the volumes on the history of the Wild West, her dog-eared copy of Byron, the book of Remington prints. He was getting to know her better through her possessions, she realized, and she had to stifle her first reaction, which was to tell him to stop.

Forcing herself to keep her mouth shut, she sank into a chair and waited for him to finish, trying to quiet her fears and calm herself, trying to get a handle on the torrent of emotions raging through her heart and soul.

He took his time, taking it all in. It was a well-worn room, comfortable and useful. He could feel the love that had filled it all these years, and for just a moment, he felt a flash of regret that he hadn't been here to share in it.

Turning at last, he looked at her. "Well, what now?" he said quietly.

She set her mouth with fierce determination. "You're leaving."

He knew what she meant and his own mouth twisted in a half smile. "There's no way in hell I'm leaving."

She drew air deep into her lungs, a last gasp of hope. "You promised."

"You trapped me into that promise under false pretenses. You never told me I had a son." His face changed. It was the first time he'd said it out loud. "A son. My God." Something very like fire lit behind his eyes.

She hardly knew him now. He was different. He was someone new. And she was very scared. Rising from the chair, she turned away, wrapping her arms around herself and closing her eyes. "The two of you hate me now, don't you?" She managed to say it calmly, coolly, as though it were just an interesting highlight on the day's events, even though every word was a knife in her soul.

He turned to stare at her, but he couldn't see her face and he didn't answer.

She was aching inside, but she would die before she let him know how bad it was. She had to get out of here before she broke down and let him see. Steeling herself, she turned back toward the kitchen. "I'm going to fix dinner," she announced, and firmly left the room.

He stared after her with conflicting emotions flashing through him, one right after another. A son. A boy who looked just like him. He should have been warned, he thought, staggered by the enormity of this new thing that had been thrust upon him. Someone should have warned him somewhere along the line.

Slowly he followed her into the kitchen, leaning against the doorjamb to watch her as she rummaged through the vegetables, looking for things to cut into pieces. She'd been through all the cupboards and had left doors open everywhere, drawers sticking out. The neat and tidy place of earlier that day was hardly recognizable. And yet, she didn't look upset. Her face was composed as she cut carrots into tiny strips. She'd had a moment of anxiety when Jimmy first left, but since then, she'd been cool as a cucumber. He frowned, watching her. Could she really be this cold? This emotionless? For just a moment he wasn't sure if maybe he didn't hate her.

After all, he hadn't asked for this. This wasn't the way it was supposed to be. You weren't supposed to be handed a bouncing baby boy of seventeen years and told, "Guess what, you're a daddy." You were supposed to start with the pregnancy. You were supposed to cherish your woman, help her through it, feel the infant move inside her. Then a baby came, something small and helpless that needed you and learned to love you because it didn't have much choice. You wanted to protect and provide for it. As it grew, you helped form its behavior, its attitudes. You taught it about your background and what you expected of it. You made it your own.

This was so different. He'd been left out of all those stages. What could he do? How could he contribute? And was there really any way to connect at this late date?

In some ways it was tempting to walk away. They'd done fine without him all these years. Jimmy had said it himself. What did they need him for now?

But he knew in his heart that it didn't matter if they needed him or not. He needed them. Now that he knew his son existed, there was no way he could turn his back.

"I can't believe you tried to hide him from me," he said at last.

She glanced up, mouth set. "I won't apologize. I wish it had worked." She sighed. "I wish Jimmy still didn't know about you and you didn't know about him. Everyone was much happier that way, don't you think?"

He shook his head slowly, trying to understand her logic and coming up empty. "Why? You don't think I have a right to my own son?"

Her green eyes flashed emerald fire. "He's not your son. You weren't here to help raise him. You have no real claim on him."

He thought that over for a moment, watching her viciously cutting vegetables to shreds.

"If I were married," she added, sounding much more collected than she looked, "and he'd grown up with another man as his father, would you still claim him?" She turned to glare at him, holding the knife high. "Well, I've been both mother and father to him. You haven't been around. What gives you the right to come in like some conquering hero all of a sudden?"

There was a wildness in her eyes and he suddenly realized she wasn't calm at all. Strangely, that reassured him. For one thing, it let him do something useful. Stepping forward firmly, he took the knife from her and laid it on the counter.

She stared at it, not sure why he'd done that, but feeling suddenly very cold.

Taking her hand, he led her to the table and sat her down in a chair, taking the chair beside hers and sitting down, as well.

"Tell me," he said serenely, "why did you name him Jimmy?"

She blinked at him, trying to focus. "I—I named him James, after my father."

He nodded. "Good choice."

She folded her hands before her on the table. "Thank you," she murmured.

"But, Shawnee..." He covered her hands with one of his own. "Why did you tell him I was dead?"

Her chin rose. "Because, to all intents and purposes, you were. I didn't think we'd ever see you again."

He shook his head, wincing. "That's crazy. I was always there. I always meant to come back. The time just got away from me."

Ah, yes, that old bugaboo, time. It must be all time's fault. She looked at him, her face a mirror of cynicism. "Would you have come back if it weren't for your sister-in-law needing this vacation? Why didn't you come on your own?"

He frowned, stung because of his own feelings of guilt. "That's not fair. I did come to find you once. I left you my address."

"Yes, but I never saw you and never got it and you had no reason to be sure that I did."

He shook his head, knowing she was right, but unable to concede the point. "I thought you were married, remember? I didn't want to get in your way. I thought for sure you would contact me if you wanted..."

She pulled her hands away from his and shifted in the chair. "It doesn't matter. We've been just fine without you."

"It matters to me." Shadows filled his eyes and the look he gave her reminded her of a cry in the wilderness, eerie and haunted. "I feel like I've been robbed."

She rose quickly, too quickly, and when she turned to go back to the cutting board, she hit her head sharply against an open cupboard door. "Oh!" she cried out, stumbling. And, like a mask of wax, her composure melted away, disappearing and leaving behind a picture of perfect misery.

Tears gushed from her eyes and she reached blindly for support. Ken's arms came around her and she couldn't refuse his comfort. "Ouch," she muttered, but it wasn't the bump on the head that had brought about the storm that flooded her. It was two days of running from reality, and finally, having reality catch her and having to deal with it.

She turned in his arms like a child, pressing her face to his chest and sobbing. He held her close and murmured nonsense words, and stroked her long, thick hair. And all the time he wondered what exactly he was holding. Was she the warm, lovely woman he'd fallen for that summer? Or someone else, someone he couldn't pin down and wasn't sure he liked at all?

With little effort, he reached around and swung her up into his arms and started for her bedroom. Still lost in sorrow, she clung to his neck and didn't ask questions. Laying her gently on the bed, he drew the coverlet up and pulled it over her shoulders.

Suddenly her eyes flew open and she started. "What...?"

Pressing her back against the pillows, he said firmly, "Come on, you'd better lie down for a while. You need some rest."

She let him push her back but she turned her face away. "You hate me," she murmured drowsily. "Don't take care of me. You hate me. I messed everything up."

He didn't answer. In some ways he agreed with her. The anger was a palpable thing inside him. He couldn't say it didn't matter, because it did. It mattered a hell of a lot.

But he cared about her. She was the mother of his child. He had to take care of her.

And despite her protests, she let him. This was a new experience for her. She was so used to doing it all herself. No one ever took care of her. She took care of other people. And yet, it felt heavenly when he tucked the covers around her and smoothed the hair back from her face. Leaning down, he kissed her forehead, and she closed her eyes

"Shawnee, you don't have to fight me anymore," he said softly. "I'm here to help you, not tear you apart."

She didn't answer, hardly heard him. Her mind was drifting already. She curled up into a ball, feeling as though all her resources had shut down, forcing her to rest, forcing her to gather her strength for self-protection. In no time at all, she was asleep.

Six

She slept fitfully, tossing and turning, but she did sleep for more than an hour. When she woke again, he was standing at the doorway of the bedroom, watching her. She had a momentary flash of pleasure before she remembered and the dread hit the bottom of her stomach again.

"Go away," she muttered from the bed.

But he didn't and she had to admit she liked the way the slow grin took over his handsome face.

"Forget it," he replied. "You need me."

"Need you!" She rose up on one elbow and glared at him, her hair flying around her head in a dark cloud. "You're dreaming."

"Someone's got to make sure you don't bump into things," he said sensibly. "You want to eat? I made some dinner."

"You did?" She shook her head, wondering if she was

still too fuzzy from sleep to get things right, peering at him suspiciously. "What did you make?"

"A sort of everything-but-the-kitchen-sink stew, something I make for myself sometimes. After all, I had to do something with all those chopped-up vegetables."

The chopped-up vegetables had been a symptom of her distress. Funny, but most of that was gone now. She still felt a tingling of unease, but nothing like the near panic of earlier in the evening.

She put a hand to her hair, smoothing it, as she looked him over. "So you can cook?" she asked, not completely convinced.

He shoved his hands into his pockets and leaned back. "You don't think I eat every meal out, do you? After all these years of living alone, I've worked up a few dishes I can fix up for myself."

She managed a wobbly smile. "Good for you," she said faintly. "Every man should at least be able to feed himself."

"Even if he has no other talents?" His grin widened. "I'll spoon up a bowl for you. You can take a look and see if you want to risk it."

She felt a smile threatening as he turned away and left her. How did he manage to make her feel warm and comforted with just a few choice comments like that? Nobody else did this to her—never had—except for him.

She got up slowly, washing up and putting on a long, yellow *holomuu* and letting her hair hang free. When she left the room, they were going to talk about Jimmy. She knew that, and she accepted that there were things Ken was going to have to know. But she was in no hurry to begin.

It was dark outside. Ken had turned on most of the lights in the living room and kitchen, and despite everything, with all the brightness and the piquant scent of stew simmering, there was a cheery atmosphere awaiting her in the main part of the house.

Ken was sitting on a stool at the bar and beside him was a bowl of his concoction. Giving him a sideways glance, she leaned over and sniffed it, and suddenly realized she was hungry, after all. She slipped onto the stool and picked up a spoon.

He watched her eat for a few minutes. Neither of them said anything, and Shawnee was grateful for his reticence. The stew was delicious, filling her with a feeling of calm, strengthening her somehow.

"What's he like?" he asked at last.

"Who?" she asked, although she knew perfectly well what he was talking about.

"Jimmy. Tell me what he's like."

A stubborn part of her didn't want to. It was as though everything she told him would be giving something away, something she would never get back again.

She took another bite and gave herself a silent lecture. After all, Ken was Jimmy's father. There was so much he'd missed, so much he would never have. He deserved whatever she could give him.

Turning, she looked into his eyes and knew he could read her mind. He knew exactly what she was thinking, and he was waiting for her to come to terms with it herself. No fussing, no prodding, no recriminations. He was giving her the space she needed. How could you hate a man like that?

"He was a good little boy," she began, then had an idea. "Do you want to see pictures?"

He shook his head. "Not yet. Just tell me."

"Okay." She thought for a moment. "He's very bright, even though he doesn't always get the best grades in school. He's good with his hands. He can whittle, or tie knots, or use tools, almost by instinct. He works with me at my restaurant about ten hours a week, or any time I need help. He's always very willing."

She stopped and frowned. This was so cut and dried, so boring. It didn't paint a true picture of her son at all. She'd better try something else.

"Do you know how in high school everyone divides up into very definite groups?" she asked him.

He nodded.

"Okay, there's the brainy group, and there's the social set who run for all the offices and run the clubs, and there are the jocks—half of whom are jerks who think they can push everyone around because they're good at sports. The other half spend part time in one of the other groups, and then there are the car kids who spend all their time working on and racing cars and trying to stay out of or falling into trouble. And finally there are the regular kids who do their homework and try to get into college or a good technical school and make up the bulk of the student population. Right?"

A smile lit his eyes. "Something like that."

"Okay. I was a regular kid most of the time, though I did hang out with the social set in my senior year. And went with a jock." She looked at him. "How about you?"

Ken grinned. "Let's see. I guess you could say I was a brainy jock who socialized a lot. How's that?"

She laughed, hit with a quick surge of delight. "That proves it. That's exactly how I would describe Jimmy." She sobered. "At least, that's how I would have described him until lately. In the last few months he's fallen in with a new set of friends." She looked down into her bowl, shaking her head. "These new guys are not people I would pick to enrich his life."

He leaned forward, interested in spite of his complete lack of background in this sort of thing. "What's wrong with them?"

"Oh, nothing really overt. They're more the car kids, and some of them are perfectly nice." Her eyes darkened. "But there are a few who seem like real punks to me. In fact, I've actually been considering selling the restaurant and moving to Honolulu in order to get him away from them."

He stared at her. He'd never been a parent before and all this intense emotion was new to him. "You would do that, upend your whole life, for him?"

"Of course. Hey, he's my son." She took another bite of stew and savored it. "I have a philosophy about raising kids," she went on, waving her spoon in the air. "I know it's not very popular these days, but I believe in it. As far as I'm concerned, if you bring a kid into this world, you're taking on a major commitment for at least the next eighteen years. That kid comes first for that length of time."

She was losing him. He shook his head, brows knit in mystification. "Wouldn't that spoil him?"

"No, you don't understand. That doesn't mean he gets anything he wants, or that he isn't taught to help me and consider my needs and feelings. But it does mean his welfare, emotional needs, education and all that come before anything else. Don't you see the difference?"

He frowned again, shaking his head slowly. "I'm not sure that I do," he said, though he was enjoying the enthusiasm she was bringing to the subject.

"Okay, look at it this way. I feel my first duty in life right now is to properly raise that kid. In another year or so I'll be able to get back to doing whatever I please to do for myself. But until this job is over, I can't." She sighed a bit dramatically and a hint of humor sparked in her eyes. "It's a commitment I've made to the propagation of the species."

He laughed. "You make it sound very portentous."

She met him with an answering smile. "It's not at all, believe me. Mostly, it's blood, sweat and tears, and a lot of hugs mixed in." She sobered. "But I won't kid you. It's hard to raise a boy without a father." She frowned, staring into space, thinking out loud. "I feel like I give it my all. I've tried to raise him right. But the world out there tugs at him and pulls at him."

He watched her, impressed. "I wish..." he began, but he didn't finish.

She didn't ask him to. She knew what he was going to say. He wished he'd been there to help her. He wished he'd been there to see Jimmy when he was young. She'd wished it, too, at one time. Now she wasn't sure what she wished.

"Tell me," he said after they'd both been silent for a few moments. "What exactly was that aberration that came and whisked..." He hesitated. It was so new and strange to him. "Whisked our son away?" he finished at last, getting the words out but feeling awkward about it. He glanced at her eyes to see if she had noticed.

She'd noticed. She half smiled, then sighed, shaking her head. "Misty. His current girlfriend."

Ken frowned, then cleared his throat pointedly. "Do you really think he should be going out with girls like that? I mean, she looked so...so..."

"Ken, he's seventeen. You just try telling a seventeen-year-old you know better than he does what sort of girl he should be going out with."

Ken raised one eyebrow."Well, I would certainly try to provide a little direction. And maybe a little discipline."

Discipline. Ha! What did he know about disciplining kids?

"Okay," she said, laying down her spoon. "Sit back and relax. I'm about to give you your first lesson in parenting a teenager."

His mouth twisted. "Should I take notes?"

"Yes," she teased. "This is important. Listen closely." She waited until he was staring with careful attention. "There is some component in the hormones of the human child that takes over at about age thirteen. Something happens that just gets worse and worse as you climb into the teen years. Hopefully, it goes away sometime in the twenties—if you're lucky. But there is no cure. Not for a teenager.''

He shook his head, half laughing. "What the hell are you talking about?''

"A deadly virus. It's called, 'anything my parents think is great, is awful,' and 'anything they tell me not to do, I'm going to do anyway.' If you really want to do something about this disease, you have to be sneaky.''

"Sneaky, huh? And how do you do that?''

"You never confront them directly about their friends or dates or what they want to do with their lives. You keep the lines of communication open and you nod and you say, 'Gee, that sounds interesting,' and you pretend to consider it thoughtfully. And then, when their guard is down, you casually point something out or make a comment that doesn't criticize, exactly, but makes them think twice or look at the situation again, on their own. It can't come from you. It has to come from them.''

He nodded slowly. "I think I get it. Say your son wants to be a boxer and you say, 'Cool,' but you go out and rent *Raging Bull* and put it on when he's in the room so he can see for himself. Right?''

"You got it." She smiled at him. "Gee, you're a quick study.''

"You think so?" He leaned closer and caught hold of her hand. "Shawnee...''

She looked into his eyes and her heart began to beat very hard. There was no denying the old attraction was still there. She responded to him, to his laughing eyes and his hard, strong hands, as she had never responded to any other man. It was thrilling. It was provocative. And it was dangerous as all hell.

"Shawnee..."

He was about to say something, do something, but she would never know what, because, at that moment, they both realized they had company.

The sound of gravel spitting filled the air and then they heard a car braking in the driveway. Shawnee jumped up, her heart in her throat. It could be Jimmy. He could be back.

But it wasn't Jimmy. It was Reggie who came running up her front steps. Reggie, followed closely by his faithful new assistant, Lani Tanaka.

"Well, congratulate me," he demanded as he burst into the room. Opening his arms wide, he grinned at Shawnee and gave her a thumbs-up. "We got the permits."

Still shaken from dashed hopes, Shawnee stared at him uncomprehendingly. "Permits?"

"To do the taping at Hamakua Point." He pulled out a sheaf of official-looking papers and waved them in the air. "We're all legal and everything, and we got it done in one day. How's that for genius?"

"How's that for connections?" Lani said quietly, mostly just to Shawnee. Her dark eyes were brimming with amusement and they seemed to see everything and know even more. "My aunt works at the board. She's a commissioner."

Shawnee smiled, liking this girl. She was still dressed as casually as she had been earlier in the day. She'd added a white baseball cap, which she wore backward, giving her the look of a teenage tomboy. She looked bright, though, much too bright to be taken in by Reggie's crazy schemes. Shawnee wondered if, after all, she should say something to her, warn her.

But Reggie hadn't noticed the mutterings in the ranks. He was much too excited. "So we can start right away," he said, enthusiasm gleaming in his eyes. "Tomorrow! We've got to get rafts and pump them up, of course. And maybe pick up some sun-block lotion. But otherwise, we're on our way.''

''Just the two of you?'' Shawnee frowned, looking from Reggie to the girl. ''Don't you need to hire a professional cameraman or something?''

Reggie waved that possible restriction away, just as he waved away most of life's little annoying verities. ''Oh, no, we're doing it all ourselves. We're using a regular little palm recorder. Works great. It's my friend's equipment, the one who got me going on this. He worked on that TV cop series they used to film here. Remember? He's a real professional.''

''Then why isn't *he* doing the taping?''

''Well...'' Reggie's face took on a pained look as though this was something he would rather not have to go into. ''You see, he's going through a personality conversion right now...''

''A what?'' Shawnee never could keep up with the latest in trendy psycho babble.

''A personality conversion. You know. He's giving up his old boarish, sexist ways and becoming a sensitive Nineties guy. And let me tell you, for him it's real hard work. He's got a lot of converting to do. He has to meet with his therapist eighteen hours a day. She's helping him purge his caveman anxieties and take on the mantle of the goddess.''

''Okay, okay,'' Shawnee said quickly, holding up her hand. She wasn't sure she could take too much more of this explanation. ''I get it. He's just not available.''

''Right.'' Reggie looked relieved that he'd made his point. ''Hey, Ken,'' he cried, noting another person in the background and stepping forward with his hand out. ''Good to see you again.''

Shawnee introduced Ken to Lani, whose eyes widened when she saw him. Glancing quickly at Shawnee, she shook hands and smiled, but didn't say a word. Shawnee hesitated, wondering if she should say something to her, then decided against it. All in good time. She began to herd them all back toward the kitchen, and as they went, Reggie sidled up to her.

"Hey, are we still married?" he asked out of the corner of his mouth.

"No, we're not," she told him wearily. "The divorce just came through this morning. Don't worry about it any longer."

A loud sigh revealed just how glad he was that was over. "What a relief." He made a face. "It's a good thing I never really got married, you know. I really hated this pretend gig you put me through. Can you imagine how bad the real thing would be?"

"I shudder to think," she said, laughing at him.

"Hey." He gave her a prod with his elbow. "Now I can approach him about investing in my project, right?"

"No, you cannot," she snapped at him. "Reggie, you just leave him alone."

He looked stricken at her attitude. "But it's such a great deal. You wouldn't want to keep a friend of yours out of it, would you? Why, you could be cheating him out of a fortune."

By now they were in the kitchen and Ken had overheard the tail end of Reggie's remarks.

"Planning on coming into a fortune, are you, Reggie?" he commented casually as he slipped onto a bar stool. "What in?"

"Reggie's got a project," Shawnee interjected quickly. "He's making a tape about…about…uh…" She couldn't bring herself to say mermaids. "About sea life off the coast. He hopes to sell it to television. But since he's never done anything like this before…"

"What do you mean? I'm ready for this like I've never been ready for anything before. I'm in love with this little project." He gestured toward the counter. "Say, Ken, I'd like a chance to get together and fill you in on what I'm doing. I figure you're the kind of man who might be interested in something like this."

"You do, do you?" Ken smiled at him. "Tell me more."

Reggie needed no further invitation. He plopped down next to Ken and leaned forward eagerly. "You see, good as this thing is, we're kind of short on financial backing. You just might see something in this if you give it a try. And if you feel like you want to throw your hat in with ours, well, hey, we'd love to have you."

Behind Reggie's back, Shawnee was shaking her head at Ken and mouthing "No way," but he grinned and told Reggie, "Sure, I'd like to hear about it. Maybe we can have lunch or something one of these days."

"Great." Reggie looked as pleased as if he'd already had an offer. "Oh, it's going to be a great adventure." He spun around on his stool. "I'm getting everyone in on it. I'm going to get Jimmy to come work for me, too."

Shawnee glanced at Lani and wondered if that smug look on her face meant that she'd had a hand in recommending Jimmy for the job. Somehow she rather thought so.

But Reggie's mind had taken a sharp turn at the thought of Jimmy. "Hey, what's going on with that son of yours, anyway?" he demanded.

She turned from where she was putting on the kettle for tea, startled. What was Reggie talking about? "Why?"

Reggie shrugged. "He passed us just a little while ago, going about a hundred and ten, hightailing it toward Hilo."

Shawnee was horrified. "A hundred and ten?"

"More like sixty," Lani told her in a quick aside, and Shawnee's tense shoulders relaxed again. Of course, Lani had to be right. That little car could no more go over a hundred than pigs could fly.

"He was going like a crazy man," Reggie insisted, waving his arms in illustration. "You'll be lucky if he comes back alive."

Shawnee turned to Lani for further reassurance.

"It wasn't really that bad," Lani told her, shaking her head.

"He wouldn't wave or say hello or nothin'," Reggie said dramatically. "He looked right at me and it was as if he was looking through me. Like I was invisible or something."

She looked at Lani, who shrugged. "That's true," she mouthed.

"Was there...was there anyone with him?" Shawnee asked, thinking about Misty.

Lani shook her head, thinking the same thing. Their gazes met, and they both knew they could communicate at will. "No. He was alone."

That, at least, was a relief. She hated to think what emotional crises did to teenagers, how they turned to one another for comfort in times of stress. She knew the dangers of that only too well. And the thought of her son with Misty chilled her blood.

She suddenly realized that Reggie was off his stool and pacing the floor, staring at Ken.

"You know," he said, as usual grabbing the attention of everyone present. "I keep wondering why you look so familiar. And now I've got it. You look exactly like Shawnee's boy, Jimmy." He looked at the other two as though he thought he'd just made a great revelation. "You've got to get the two of them together, Shawnee. They'll be stunned. They won't believe the resemblance."

Ken glanced at Shawnee and gave an almost imperceptible shrug. "You know, Reggie, I've met Jimmy. And I've seen the resemblance."

"Oh." Reggie did a double take. "Oh, I see," he said, though he still didn't, because next he asked, "What are you, Jimmy's uncle or something?"

"No. No, I'm not his uncle." Ken glanced at Shawnee again, waiting to see how she wanted to handle this.

"Uh-oh." Reggie looked from one to the other of them, squinting as though he were sure to figure this out any moment. But then his face went blank. "Then I don't get it," he said, truly stumped. "What's going on?"

Shawnee hesitated. Why couldn't she just come on out and tell everyone? After all, it was as plain as the noses—and everything else—on their faces. She could see from Lani's expression that she already got the connection. If only Reggie didn't have to have everything explained to him seven times.

"Oh, Reggie," she said, exasperation ringing in her voice.

"What did I do now?" he asked, looking around quickly and looking so much like a guilty child she had to laugh.

"Not a thing. It's only that…you're making me say it out loud."

"What?"

"Ken is Jimmy's father. Can't you see it?"

"Wait a minute." He shook a finger at her, as though she'd forgotten something. "Jimmy's father is dead."

"Reggie, please. That was a story I told Jimmy so he wouldn't feel abandoned by his father."

"Oh. I see." He stared at her as if she'd gone crazy. "Having his father dead was supposed to be better than having him someplace else, huh?" He shook his head, his face a mirror of skepticism. "I don't know if that was such a good trade-off."

Shawnee had to work hard to keep defensiveness out of her voice. "I had to do something and that was the decision I made at the time."

Reggie pounded his own chest with his fist. "Why didn't you ask my help? I could have helped you think up a better story than that."

She was so, so tired. Was she going to have to go through all this with every one of her relatives? "I'm sure you could have. But the fact is, that is the story I told."

"Uh-huh." He glanced suspiciously at Ken.

He still wasn't clear on the details, that much was certain. She looked at him and then at Lani and decided a full explanation was in order. "The truth is that Ken and I lost touch with each other before the baby was born. Ken never knew I was pregnant. I didn't know how to find him. Now he's come back and..."

"He's Jimmy's father, all right," Reggie decided after giving it careful scrutiny. He frowned thoughtfully. "Does Jimmy know about this?"

"He just found out today."

"So that's why he was racing down the highway." His face changed. "Hey, maybe we'd better go find him. God knows what he might be doing."

Before Shawnee could answer that, the telephone rang. She paled and went to it quickly, praying it wouldn't be the highway patrol telling her there'd been an accident.

It wasn't. Instead, it was an old friend who had worked as a waitress in the café. Nowadays, she helped her husband run a bar on the outskirts of Hilo.

"Shawnee, honey? Your son just came in here and tried to use a fake ID to get himself a drink."

Shawnee gasped. That wasn't like Jimmy at all. *"What?"*

"Arnie's got him in the back and he's talking to him, just kind of kidding him along, but I thought you'd want to come and get him. He seems to be real upset about something."

"Thanks, Mele," she said breathlessly. "I'll be there right away."

Dropping the phone back in its cradle, she turned to the others. They were all staring, waiting to hear what she'd reacted to so strongly. Seeing her face, Ken slipped off his stool and came to her.

"What is it, Shawnee?" he asked. "What's happened?"

In a monotone, she told them all what Mele had told her. Then she turned to get her jacket. "I've got to go get him," she said. "I'll be back as soon as ..."

"No." Ken had her arm in the grip of his strong hand and he swung her around to face him. "You stay here. I'll go."

She stared up at him, bewildered. "You? You can't go. You ... you're the reason he's so upset."

"That's why I'm the one who has to go." He touched her chin with his thumb, his eyes deep as caverns. "I'm going, Shawnee. Whether you like it or not. So give me the address of this place and let me get going."

She wasn't sure what she should do. She looked toward Reggie for help, but he was already scribbling down the address for Ken and explaining how to find the place.

She found herself trailing him to the door, still protesting. At the last minute, he turned and dropped a quick kiss on her lips.

"Shawnee," he said softly, his gaze holding hers, "the whole weight of this isn't just on your shoulders anymore. You don't have to do it all alone." And then he was taking the stairs two at a time and going for his car.

She stared after him, watching his athletic stride, watching the way the moonlight played on his hair, and not sure whether the feeling coursing through her was relief ... or resentment.

Seven

"Mom? Hey, Mom, are you asleep?"

She woke up with a start to find her son sitting on her bed, staring down at her, his eyes red and bleary, still dressed as he had been the night before. It was obvious he hadn't been to sleep himself, even though sunlight was streaming in through the blinds.

She hadn't meant to fall asleep herself. She'd spent the long lonely hours of the previous night pacing the floor and worrying about where Ken and Jimmy were and what they were doing. The last thing she remembered was looking at the clock and thinking three o'clock was awfully late and where the hell were they, anyway? And now this.

"What is it?" she said, half rising and trying to clear her brain. "What's the matter?"

"Nothing," he replied in a voice that said "Everything." "I'm going to go to bed and I needed . . ." His voice trailed off.

"What?" She reached out and touched his arm, loving him so, aching for the hurt she wished he'd never had to suffer. "You look half dead."

He flexed his shoulders and grimaced. "Yeah, I'm really tired."

"Where have you been?"

"Driving. Ken and I...we drove around the island." His short laugh wasn't mirthful at all.

"Oh." She couldn't tell if that was good or bad. Nothing about his expression gave it away. Had they fought the whole time? Had he given Ken the silent treatment? Oh, he was very good at the silent treatment. It had her climbing the walls every time he used it on her. Or had something good actually happened? Had they talked out the situation and come to an understanding? Did she dare hope for that?

"Did you just get back?"

"Yeah." He stretched and yawned. "Ken's going to sleep on our couch."

"Oh. Okay." There was no resentment in his face. No anger. What did that mean? She wished she could come right out and ask him, but right now she didn't want to do anything to tip the balance. At least he was home. At least he was safe.

"Mom...I just..." He shook his head and didn't go on.

"What is it, darling?" She reached out to touch him again. He looked so tired, so young. She remembered when he'd been little and had called her into his room again and again, complaining about monsters at the window. She'd finally realized the branches of a tree outside his room were scratching against the side of the house, making an eerie sound that was scaring him. Knowing she couldn't get the tree trimmed until morning, she'd sat on his bed and told him stories about his great-great-grandfather, the pirate Morgan Caine, and how he'd heard the sea witch clawing at his cabin door during a storm at sea...

"He was so scared, he tried to hide under his bed, but there was a cold wind blowing down there and it almost froze him, so he climbed back up and tried to hide in his closet, but there was a hole in the bottom of his closet and he almost fell through and was swept out to sea. The clawing sound went on and on and there was no place left to hide, so he finally called on all his courage and opened his door to confront the sea witch and get it over with. And guess what. It wasn't the sea witch at all, but a beautiful, half-drowned Polynesian princess. He brought her inside and nursed her back to health and fell in love and married her, and she became your great-great-great-grandmother."

"Wow."

"Now, what do you think about that scratching outside right now?" she'd asked Jimmy, who had listened to the whole story, wide-eyed. "You thought it was a monster when you first heard it. But what if it's a princess?"

Jimmy had shaken his head solemnly. "Uh-uh," he'd said. "It's the sea witch. Pirate Morgan Caine didn't get her, so she's still out there, isn't she?"

She had to laugh every time she thought of that incident. Jimmy did have a way of seeing the dark side of things. And whenever she tried to comfort him, she never seemed to get it exactly right.

"What do you need?" she asked him now. "What can I do for you?"

His eyes were so deep and so black in this light, with dark smudges underneath, making them look huge. "I don't know. I'm so... I'm really confused."

A lump rose in her throat. "Of course, you are," she whispered, patting him, trying to soothe him with her hand. "It's only natural." She curled her fingers around his wrist. She wanted to pour it all out to him, all the pain and indecision she'd gone through herself, all the heartache, all the love. But there was that huge lump in her throat and she just couldn't do it. "I'm so sorry, darling," she whispered simply. "So very sorry."

"No, Mom." His face twisted. "I want something from you, Mom. I want you to tell me something."

"What?" She touched his cheek and tried to search his eyes. "What?" Anything. Anything at all. She was desperate to blot out the pain in his face.

"I—I don't know what," he said brokenly, his face stricken. "I just have this feeling that I need you to tell me something, and I don't know what it is."

She stared at him, wishing more than anything that she knew what it was he needed. "I love you," she said, knowing that wasn't it but trying anyway.

He bit his lip and started to say something, then stopped and nodded instead. "I love you, too, Mom," he said huskily. "I really do."

Her eyes filled with tears. "You don't hate me?" she asked, her voice barely a whisper.

His arms came around her and he hugged her tightly. "I could never hate you, Mom. You know that."

No, she didn't know that. She'd hoped, she'd prayed, but she didn't know it.

He drew away suddenly, as though he'd remembered he was too old for this hugging stuff. "I guess I'll go to bed," he muttered, rising and turning away. "See you later."

And he was gone.

She got up slowly and dressed, making her way to the living room. There was Ken, just as Jimmy had said, sound asleep on her couch. She stood over him for a moment, studying the lines of his face. Harsh and angular now, they had once been curved and muted. A playful dimple had become a somewhat cynical crease, an arched brow was now hard and rugged. The boy had become the man. But what kind of man was he really? Enough of a man to be a father to her son?

She sank to the coffee table and sat watching him, remembering and renewing, and as she watched, the rigidity seemed to soften and the hard lines began to curve, but she knew it was she who was changing, not him. He was still the same. She was letting her feelings overpower her rationality. And she couldn't afford to do that.

Rising abruptly, she shook him by the shoulder.

"Huh?" He resisted, then opened one eye a tiny sliver. "What?"

"Come on. I can't leave you out here for visiting neighbors to gawk at," she said briskly. "You'd better go in and sleep on my bed."

He didn't really wake up, but he got up, and she half led, half pushed him into her room and down onto the bed. Keeping her mind blank, as though she were working with a patient in a hospital bed, she removed his shoes and his belt and loosened his pants. He grunted once, and rolled over on command, but for all intents and purposes, he was asleep. She pulled the covers over him and finally let herself look down at his handsome face, the hair rumpled and falling over his forehead, the mouth soft and vulnerable in sleep, and suddenly a wave of emotion filled her and she had to choke back a sob and leave as quickly as possible, closing the door firmly and telling herself, "You are not to go back in there. You hear?"

But as she walked slowly to the kitchen, she had to laugh. What a ridiculous situation to be in. She had a man in her bed and she didn't know what to do with him.

She cleaned the kitchen and called the café to make sure everything was running smoothly, paid some bills and did a load of laundry, and then sat and stared at the ocean, letting the sunlight sparkling on the tiny whitecaps hypnotize her, trying not to think, but thinking all the while.

She'd just about made up her mind to go for a swim when she heard Jimmy moving about. Jumping up, she went to his room.

"What are you doing?" she cried upon finding him dressed and ready to go out. "You haven't had nearly enough sleep."

"Hi, Mom." He looked up and smiled at her, his face bright and rested. Just a few hours of rest seemed to have worked a miracle. He looked very like he always did. "I've got to get out of here," he said, reaching for his wallet and shoving it into the back pocket of his jeans.

"Wait a minute," she said, unsure of his motives and nervous, considering everything that had been going on for the past twenty-four hours. "Where are you going?"

He turned and looked at her in surprise. "Don't you remember? Both your busboys are taking off to go deep-sea fishing today. I promised I'd fill in for them."

"Oh, that's right." She laughed ruefully and shook her head. "Jimmy, you're so responsible sometimes, it's almost scary. Thanks for remembering."

Throwing her a cheery wave, he was out of the house before she realized she hadn't taken a moment to wring any more information out of him. She still had no idea what he thought of Ken, or how he was feeling about coming face-to-face with the father he'd thought was dead.

But he didn't seem to be holding a grudge against her. She sighed with relief and her heart filled with love for him. What a good boy he was, despite everything. What a wonderful boy.

She went back out and flipped through a magazine, managing to contain herself for almost an hour before she could stand it no longer. She had to go in and talk to Ken.

Barging right into the bedroom, she swung up and sat herself cross-legged on the bed beside him.

"I can't wait any longer," she announced to his still-sleeping form. "I have to find out what you two talked about on your long trek around the island."

The lazy lump beneath the covers barely stirred. "Talked about?" He blinked at her sleepily, his eyes unfocused. "Who? Where?" he muttered just before diving beneath the covers with a groan and pulling them over his head.

"You know who I mean," she said, yanking the covers away and forcing him to face the day. "Jimmy."

"Jimmy who?"

"Ken!"

He sighed, squinting his eyes against the light. "It's too early."

She loved the way he looked, like a rather handsome mole, reluctantly facing sunshine. "Actually, it is very, very late. Now give."

Throwing her a baleful look, he tried to comply. "We didn't talk about much of anything. We're both pretty quiet, you know. Neither one of us is a real chatty guy."

"Oh, come on." She nudged him with her foot. "You can do better than that. Give me what I want and I'll let you go back to sleep."

"Okay, let's see." He yawned and leaned back, eyes drifting shut until she prodded him again. "Okay, okay. We talked about... let me see." He levered himself up so that he was resting against the pillows, half sitting and slowly coming awake. "We talked about the best kinds of tires to use on street-legal race cars. We talked about how the Dodgers are doing this year and why Hawaii doesn't have its own major league team. We talked about your restaurant. He recited the menu to me."

Was it just her imagination, or did men seem to have the most boring conversations on record? "Oh, brother. Didn't you talk about anything substantive?"

He raised an eyebrow and sniffed. "I think men and women may have a slight disagreement over what is substantive. You know what I mean?" But he grinned at her. "Still, you might like this one. We did talk about who on the island makes the best chocolate malted."

Right. She was dying to know. "Oh, yeah? And who does?"

"Marie's All-Nite Diner in Kona. We stopped by and had one." His eyelids drifted down as he let the memory linger. "Smooth as satin going down. She makes it with a chocolate syrup..."

Shawnee threw up her hands. "Didn't you talk about us? Or about him? Or about how he feels?"

He shook his head, then seemed to remember something. "We did talk about Misty."

Not what she'd hoped for. "Oh, brother," she repeated, realizing the wrong words said about Misty could be disastrous. She certainly didn't want Jimmy running off to marry the girl just to show the rest of them he could do whatever he pleased. "What did you say?" she asked apprehensively.

His face took on superior airs. "I was very careful. I took your lesson to heart and I played it very cool."

"Yeah, I'll bet." He was being cute, but she was resisting it. "So give. What did you say? Did you lecture him about good girls and bad girls?"

He looked offended. "I didn't lecture. I said she was a really cute girl. I said I bet he got a lot of envy from his friends for going with her, and he agreed that, yes, he did."

She groaned. "Wonderful. You promoted her. I thought you wanted to kill this romance."

"Hold on. I did just what you advised. Without saying anything bad about her at all, I added that I hoped someday he would find a girl like the girl his mother was at that age."

"What?" Shawnee gaped at him in horror. "What teenage boy wants a girl like his mother?"

"You'd be surprised. I told him I hoped he would find a girl like you, someone who had your warmth, your understanding, your ability to listen and to really hear things." His voice slowed and deepened. "Your talent for making connections and keeping them safe." Reaching out, he ran his fingers over the inside of her ankle, gazing at it as though it interested him somehow. "I told him I hoped he would find a feeling like we had." He looked into her eyes. "Remember?"

"Yes. I remember." Suddenly she shivered, but she didn't push his hand away. "I'll never forget."

Slowly she leaned back against the pillows, right next to him. "The sun was so hot on my skin that day," she mused softly, her eyes unfocused as she let memory take over for the moment. "And the water felt so cool."

"And you were so soft," he murmured, turning to capture her chin in his big hand. "Just as soft as you are now."

She felt soft. She felt as though she were made of something so soft it would melt in the sun, and she melted against him as he kissed her. And all she knew was that her softness was ready to meld with his hardness and it had been ready for eighteen years.

But she couldn't let it. She'd been so good and strong so far, she couldn't let it all go to waste now. Making love all those years ago with Ken had launched her life in the direction it had taken. She had no idea what making love with him now would do, but she knew it just might change everything, and she wasn't sure she could handle that.

Still, it was very tempting to give in to the fire that was licking deep inside her, spreading heat down her legs, making her ache for his touch. If only...

"Ken," she murmured against his lips. "I'd better..."

"No." He turned, still drowsy but resolute. "You'd better stay right here and keep me company." Lazily, he nipped at her earlobe. "This bed has been too lonely too long."

She laughed softly, deep in her throat. "How do you know that?" she demanded, but she couldn't help but arch her neck to his tickling kisses, sighing as they sent shock waves through her system. "You mean you haven't heard about the orgies I hold here?"

His tongue made a faint curlicue at her hairline. "You can hold all the orgies you want," he muttered against her skin. "But if I'm not here, they don't mean a thing and you know it."

"Oh, really?" His mock arrogance made her laugh. "You really do think I've spent most of my life just waiting for you to come back, don't you?"

"Yes." Suddenly he seemed very serious. "And I've spent most of my life preparing to come back. Can't you tell?"

She didn't really believe him, but she loved what he was saying, anyway. His mouth found hers and she opened to him, enjoying the slight rasp of his tongue, soaking up his heat, turning so that her body could touch his all up and down the length between them. For just a moment more she would let this happen. Not for long, but for just a moment or two more...

"I should go," she whispered, but he pulled her closer.

"No," he said again. "You should stay." He kissed her temple, her ear, her neck in quick succession, and his hard hands slipped beneath her sweater and made a tantalizing impression on her back, the fingers digging in just enough to excite her, the palms rubbing as though she were made of fine silver.

"You should stay and make love," he murmured against her skin, pressing his face into the curve of her shoulder. "It's something that needs to be done."

She smiled, even though she knew she was being tempted to do something that was just as crazy now as it had been before. But she smiled and laughed softly, and when he unhooked her bra and shoved back her sweater and took both her breasts in his hands, she arched her back and caught her breath at the suddenness of the sensation that swept through her like lightning, shocking and provoking at the same time, and suddenly she knew it was too late to back out.

She knew she should push herself out of his arms and run for cover, but she didn't want to do that, couldn't do it, couldn't even imagine doing it. Suddenly she wanted him more than she'd ever wanted anything else in her life, wanted him hard and hot and now . . . now.

"Ken," she cried out, her eyes wide with surprise. "Oh, quickly!"

He tried, but there were certain things that had to be done—like getting her out of the shorts that seemed to cling like Velcro. He tugged at the zipper, then swore obscenely as it stuck. She helped him, peeling away the cloth as though it were smothering her. His own shirt was easy enough, but his jeans were button-fly and the way her hands were shaking, there was no way she could release them. He did it himself with one impatient jerk, and then they were both free, skin on skin, his hard strength against her soft acceptance.

He was so beautiful. He'd been beautiful that day, his firm flesh shimmering in the sunlight, but this was better. This was real, not a memory. She reached for him, stroking and savoring the feel of him, wanting to somehow possess him in ways she couldn't fathom, needing to hold him as though he were as much a spiritual being as a physical one.

He quivered at her touch and reached for her, needing to feel her beneath him, needing to find his place between her legs, to reach for the heat that would sustain him, to reach for the fulfillment that he had lacked all these years. Pausing only to secure protection for them both, he came to her as conqueror as well as conquered.

There was a growl starting deep inside her, a primal, demanding sound that she'd never made before, never knew she was capable of. But she wanted him with a fierce desire that blinded her to anything else.

The sound came out and she wrapped herself around him, driving him inside, urging him to catch the rhythm she alone could set, and then he was there, with her, joined as one, and they found what they were searching for in the fast give and take that happened between their bodies as it happened between their souls.

It was over much too fast, and yet it seemed to last forever. She lay, panting, wondering if she could survive without him when he left. She knew she shouldn't have done this, shouldn't have set herself up for more heartbreak. But now that she'd done it, she was glad. She loved him. She would always love him. And this was probably the only way she would ever be able to tell him so.

"Wow," he murmured sleepily. "What just happened here? Did I miss it?"

Rolling over, she faked a punch to his arm. "You could at least say something romantic," she told him. "Something about how you've never known anyone like me before."

"I've never known anyone like you before." He rose above her and there was nothing but sincerity in his eyes. "Before, or after," he murmured, and he began kissing her again, her mouth, her nose, her chin, and then lower, capturing one nipple and then the other and teasing them until her hips began to move again and she moaned.

"I thought there was more where that came from," he said with a smile. "Only this time, let's go slow enough to notice when it comes."

They went very slowly, exploring and touching and kissing, backing off when the heat began to rise, until finally, they made slow, perfect love, holding each other in an embrace that seemed to last forever.

And Shawnee let it happen. She closed her mind to doubts and anxieties. For once, she would let herself go and drink in all the love and pleasure she could find in the day. Just for once. Because that was the pattern of her life. She had to wait a long time for her second chances.

Eight

"**I** like him."

Shawnee sat stock still and cross-legged on her floor and stared at him. "Really?" she said breathlessly, because this was so very important. She had to hear it again. Many times. "You really do?"

Ken nodded his head slowly. "I really do." He grinned and settled back against the pillows on her couch. "And he hasn't actually tried to be congenial to me so far. He hasn't been nasty, but he hasn't gone out of his way to be friends."

She looked down at the mug of tea that she'd set down on the coffee table and closed her hands around it. Her heart was filled with joy and tears were threatening to brim her eyes. She couldn't face him or she would lose it for sure. It took a moment before she could be certain that her voice would be steady. "He'll get better once he's more used to this," she said at last.

"Sure." Ken watched her, watched the emotions in her face and marveled at how easily he could read her. There had never been any other woman in his life that he could read this way. Or maybe, he thought suddenly, there had never been another woman that he'd bothered to watch this closely.

She loved her son with a love that was fierce and beautiful. He wasn't sure he would ever love Jimmy that way. But he liked seeing it in her.

"When I first saw him... Shawnee, I thought I was dreaming. I thought... I didn't know what to think. My mind sort of went into fog mode and I put myself on automatic for a while. I just couldn't believe it. That I could have a grown son like that. It was incredible. It still is."

She nodded. "I didn't know what you would do."

"I never dreamed he existed. The possibility never entered my mind."

"So what did you think? Once you'd accepted it, I mean."

He thought for a moment. "I was angry and confused at first. I felt like you'd lied to me, held out on me. It took a while to put it all together and see that there wasn't much else you could have done. And inside..." He gazed at her honestly. "Shawnee, it still hurts to know he's been alive all these years and I didn't know it."

She winced. "You're still mad at me."

He nodded slowly. "A part of me is. It's not fair, I know, but I can't help it."

She smiled a little sadly, looking down into her tea. "And a part of me has always been furious with you for not knowing—not being able to sense—that I needed you."

He nodded. "Sure. Why not?"

She lifted her face to look at him. Their gazes met and held, and something passed between them. She could almost see it, a wisp of understanding, a bond of knowing, caring, an unspoken communication so basic it filled her with a warm sense of belonging that she'd never felt before. Silently she held out her hand. Still holding her gaze, he took it, and for a moment they sat very still, until a spark of humor entered the mix, and they both began to laugh softly. Leaning forward, he kissed her mouth and she closed her eyes and thought she must know what a flower felt like when the sun touched it.

"Tell me what it was like," he said, sitting back again. "Tell me about how you first found out you were pregnant. What you thought." His lopsided grin was slightly ironic. "How you hated me."

She told him—starting with the morning he'd left with the rest of his team, when she'd tried so hard to make it to the airport to see him off, but couldn't get her uncle's car started, and then hitched a ride that took her to every backwoods village between home and Hilo, only to miss his flight.

"I thought you'd just decided not to come," he told her. "Remember how you teased me about that? About how you didn't like goodbyes?"

She shook her head. "It wasn't that at all. I tried to get there. I was in shock when I got to the airport and found you'd already gone." She bit her lip as the memory of that day came sweeping back. "There was so much we still had to tell each other, so much we hadn't said. I didn't even know where you lived in California. I wasn't even sure how to spell your last name." She sighed. "And then I was so sure you would write."

He shook his head, annoyed at that young version of himself, but curiously resigned at the same time. He knew himself. This was what he was like. There was no point getting all worked up over it.

"I never write," he told her ruefully. "I tried to call you a couple of times, but I didn't have the right number. I kept getting someone speaking Japanese. And then I gave up on that, because I had plans to come back in the summer. Remember? I'd promised you that. I thought it was just a matter of time."

"And in the meantime," she said, eyes shining with unshed tears. "I realized a baby would be here before you would."

She told him about her original panic, and how she'd come to accept what had happened. About how she had counted the days until the first day of summer, sure she would be seeing him again. About how long she clung to hope.

"He was the most perfect baby," she told him, and got out the photo albums. They spent an hour poring over them. "Jimmy was my joy, right from the beginning. I never, ever regretted having him." She looked at Ken, her gaze clear. "I hope you don't regret it, either," she said softly.

He looked at her with the same open expression. "Never," he said firmly. "But how did you make it all this time? Financially, I mean."

"It was hard at first. I had to take a lot of help from relatives, and that wasn't easy. Not that they begrudged me. But I hate to owe, you know? But once I started working in the café, everything was pretty good. I could take Jimmy with me. The place has been in my family for years and I got help in buying part of it from relatives. Now I'm the sole owner. It makes a tidy little income during tourist season."

"I'm glad. Glad you've been all right, glad you've done such a good job with your café." He sighed, looking at her in all candor. "I have to admit, that makes me feel a little better about having left you alone all these years."

"You didn't know."

"No." She was trying to let him off the hook and that was very nice, but he shouldn't let her do it. "But I could have tried harder to find you," he admitted. "I shouldn't have given up just because your brother said you were married. I should have gone looking for you and heard it from your own lips."

She shrugged and smiled at him. "That's all water under the bridge. It's over. We've got to get on with life."

He hesitated, his gaze clouding. "Tell me the truth. How do you really think Jimmy's handling it?"

"His father being alive and well and sitting in his house?" She laughed softly. "He's having problems with it. That's only natural. But I think he'll come through okay. I think he's already healing. When he left for work he seemed fine. I know that doesn't necessarily mean anything permanent. But it is a sign."

He nodded slowly, thinking that over, and she looked out the window, not wanting to show him how worried she really was. She hoped she wasn't being too optimistic when she told him things would be all right, but she didn't know. Jimmy had looked all right when he'd left for work, but earlier, when they'd first come back from their ride around the island, he hadn't looked all right at all. His sleep had helped to settle him down, but she knew that pain was still inside him. And how was it going to manifest?

As if on cue, Jimmy's car could be heard arriving in the driveway, and in a moment, he was bounding up the steps. As he walked in the door, his face hardened when he saw Ken sitting on the couch. He looked at him without greeting him, and then he looked at his mother.

"I'm going to change and go on over and get Misty," he said shortly. "We're going to the movies."

Obviously her hopes had been a little too high. He wasn't ready to accept things as yet. He was still angry. Well, she could hardly blame him. But she had to try to get him to see the whole picture and not just his part in it. Rising, she went to him.

"Jimmy, please come and sit with us for a few minutes," she said. "We need to talk."

He hesitated and she could tell he dreaded this, would do almost anything to avoid it. But at last he shrugged and said, "Sure," and came with her to sit in a chair opposite his father. His body language was bristling with No Trespassing signs, but at least he was there.

"What do you want?"

Now that she had him here, she had no idea what she really wanted to say to him. "Just love your father" was the message she needed to convey, but you couldn't tell a kid to just do anything and expect it to happen.

"We've got to talk this out, Jimmy," she said, then winced, knowing she was being evasive and regretting the way she'd put that.

And just as she'd feared, he took the opening she'd set up for him. "What for?" he said, his tone laced with a touch of sarcasm. "We've already talked about it. I understand everything." He waved a hand in Ken's direction. "He's my long, lost father and he's back. We took a ride last night and got to know each other. That's all there is to it. I don't need therapy or anything like that. I can handle it."

She glanced at Ken for help but he was looking as lost as she felt. Turning back to her son, she tried hard for a wisdom that just wouldn't come. "That's not all there is to it, Jimmy," she said, then had a thought about something else that was missing from his picture of things. She sat forward, imploring him with her eyes at the same time she tried to find the right words to explain things to him.

"There's so much more you just don't understand. You don't know who we were then, Ken and I. You don't know why..." She bit her lip. How could she explain this? "There are the human feelings behind it all, the context in which it happened, the reasons why..."

Jimmy stiffened, eyes wide, and for just a second she saw the panic there again. "I don't want to know any reasons why," he said quickly. Then his face hardened, his eyes burning, and he added cruelly, "I mean ... everybody already knows the reasons why people shack up with each other."

Shawnee's head snapped back as though he'd slapped her. "Jimmy!" she cried, wounded in a way she'd never expected to be hurt by her son.

But before she even had the name out, Ken was up and hauling Jimmy out of his chair with one hand twisted in his shirt, his face hard with fury.

"Don't you ever ... *ever* ... talk to your mother like that again," he said in a voice that could have cut diamonds.

Jimmy's eyes blazed defiantly. They stared at one another for a long moment, Jimmy's young insolence to Ken's strong sense of command. Shawnee held her breath.

"Sorry, Mom," Jimmy muttered at last, though he didn't look much like a penitent.

Ken let go and Jimmy dropped down into the chair, but in less than a beat he was up again and striding for the door.

"Jimmy," Shawnee called. "Come back."

He didn't acknowledge her call in any way, and in another moment he was out on the beach, running along the edge of the water.

"I'll go after him," Ken said quickly.

She turned, her hand on his arm. They'd botched it, that was for sure, but she didn't know what to do to fix things. "No," she said quickly. "I'd better go."

Ken was shaking his head, pushing away her hand. "No. He doesn't need babying. He needs to get a few things straight."

She stared at him, shocked. "What are you saying?" she demanded. "I think I know best how to handle him. He's my son."

He looked down at her coolly. "Shawnee, he's my son, too. I have a right to have some say in what happens to him and what he's thinking."

She resented his words, had a visceral reaction to them she couldn't put into words. "You weren't here..." she began vaguely, fading as she realized what she was about to say.

"That's right. I wasn't here, and I'll always regret it. If I'd known, I would have been here. But that can't be helped now. It's over."

Was it over? And would he have been here if he'd known? She didn't know if she could believe that.

Ken started for the door again, determined to go after Jimmy. She followed, pulling on his arm. "Do you really think you should go after him?" she asked him anxiously. "Maybe he needs time to think."

"He's had time to think," Ken said shortly. "What he needs is some information to think with."

She caught at his hand, not letting him leave, torn with anxiety, yet unsure of what to do next.

"What do you mean?"

He covered her hand with his own and smiled down into her distressed eyes. "He needs to know how it was, Shawnee," he told her. "He needs to understand what a special person his mother was in those days."

Her brow was furrowed with worry. "Ken, I don't think..."

"This is my place, Shawnee. I'm the only one who can tell him." He pulled away from her and went toward the door. "I'm going to catch him and make him listen to me. You stay here. I'll be back soon."

She watched him go, her heart in her throat. Single motherhood was tough, but this was even tougher, and she was beginning to have doubts about the chances for survival.

* * *

"Run for it."

There was a tiny part of his mind, a very ugly, embarrassing corner of his brain, whispering that in his ear.

"Run for it. Get in your car and take off. Go back to the mainland. Forget all this. Who needs these things complicating your life?"

He wasn't proud of that little voice, but he couldn't deny that it was there. Still, he didn't have to listen to it. As he jogged along the beach, looking for Jimmy, he pushed it away and tried to concentrate on what he was going to say to the boy when he found him.

His son. He still wasn't used to the concept. And yet, what he'd seen in Jimmy's face back at the house, when he'd been so angry, had been like looking in the mirror. He remembered how that felt, that consuming rage, that anger at parents, at the people who brought you into the world. He'd felt it himself. He'd been so full of fury that summer when he'd come to Hawaii, he'd thought he would never have a day without the rage churning in him again.

Funny to look back on it now. He'd come out of that black hole and never gone back in. And the only reason he'd come out was because he'd met Shawnee.

The summer of his seventeenth year had been part heaven, part hell. First, after a season of fighting hard against bigger water polo players and an unreasonable coach, he'd hung in and worked his way to the top, making the all-star team that was scheduled to go to Hawaii to a big tournament. He'd thought he was on top of the world, but he'd come down fast when his parents had called him in for a family conference and informed him they were getting a divorce.

"It's the best answer for all of us," his solemn father had said. "You want us to be happy, don't you?"

No, he hadn't particularly cared if his parents were happy or not. That wasn't the point. They were supposed to be *parents,* damn it. They were supposed to be there for him, not off looking for some sort of "happiness." What right did they have to tear apart his world? He'd reacted with anger and hostility. His grades had dive-bombed and he'd gotten into fights at school. He was almost suspended from the team, but he wrote a letter of apology to the dean and got a reprieve. By the time he'd left for Hawaii, he was trouble waiting to happen.

And happen it did with a fight in the very first game of the tournament. This time the suspension held. He was out. He was supposed to spend all his time sulking in the hotel room, but the team was always gone, playing exhibition games when the tournament play was over. And Ken wandered into Hiroshi's store that fateful afternoon, and met Shawnee Caine.

"Hey, Jimmy! Wait up."

There he was, just ahead. He turned and watched Ken approach, his face sullen, and Ken's heart started beating a little faster. He had to get this right. He owed it to Shawnee, above all. He owed it to Jimmy, too. But how was he going to explain to him what had happened that summer? How was he going to tell him that his mother had saved an angry boy from becoming an angry man? That when she'd made love with him, she hadn't done it in a fit of teenage lust. Her lovemaking had been an act of healing, pure and simple. She'd done it to save Ken's soul. And in the process, together they'd created a miracle. Could he find the words to tell this boy how it had been? He had to. There was no alternative.

Shawnee watched them walking across the sand, side by side but not touching one another. They were almost the same height. Ken was just a little taller. It made her heart leap to see them together this way.

For just a moment she let herself dwell on how this felt. Ken was back. She hadn't really allowed herself to take in the full import of this situation. For so long she'd prayed for him to return and be a part of their lives. Then she'd accepted that he was never coming, and finally, decided it would be a disaster if he did come. But all of that was over now, because he was here.

He wasn't here to marry her and carry her off to a life of happily-ever-after. She was too grounded in reality to even think such a thing. But he was here and he was worth knowing, worth having back, even if for just a short while. Jimmy might not be able to recognize it now, but someday he would be glad he'd met his father, glad to know what sort of man he was.

Her heart was full. She could ask for a lot more than what she was getting, but she was no whiner. One thing she had learned was that you couldn't dictate happiness, you couldn't make people act the way you would like them to act. They did what they felt was best for themselves, and she had to do likewise. She was going to enjoy what she could and live her life the way it had to be led.

Ken and Jimmy had reached the steps to the house when she turned and escaped into the kitchen. She knew Ken had talked to Jimmy, but she had no idea what had been said, and she didn't want to stand there waiting, trying to read faces. Humming a cheerful tune, she began wiping down counters, hoping for the best.

"It's okay," Ken said from the doorway. "You can cut out the act. He's gone to take a shower."

The humming died in her throat and she sagged against the counter, throwing down the dishrag. "How is he?" she asked anxiously. "What did you say to him?"

He came toward her slowly, taking her in his arms.

"I told him about how you saved me from drowning in my own misery way back when," he said, pressing a kiss at her temple. "I reminded him that you'd practically had to raise your three brothers with very little help from your parents, that you were always there for everyone, including me, including Jimmy. That it was about time he took a good look at what you do for other people."

She sighed, shaking her head. "I'm sure he appreciated the lecture."

"He understood perfectly what I was trying to say. Believe it or not, we speak the same language. He's going to be okay."

Reaching down, he found her mouth with his and began to explore it. She kissed him back, wrapping her arms around his neck and arching her body into his. This was what she had missed all these years, the simple comfort of body contact. Right now she was planning to get in all that she could, because as soon as Ken left, she was in for another dry spell, and she knew it.

Jimmy's shower lasted a long, long time, but when he came out he was almost normal, treating her casually and being formal but not unkind to Ken. There was no further mention of going out with Misty. He and Ken chatted and Shawnee watched them, her heart full of love for them both.

Ken went back to investigating her shelves, and as he looked through things he found a trophy and read the label.

"You're a swimmer," he said, smiling at Jimmy, who nodded but didn't reply. "I was a swimmer, too. You have to be if you're going to play water polo." He gestured toward the trophy. "Pretty good times. Do you want to swim in college?"

"Maybe."

They discussed colleges and where the best swim coaches were, and Shawnee watched, knowing Ken was working hard at finding places where he could connect with his son, things they could find in common. How could she ever have dreaded them meeting face-to-face? Ken was everything Jimmy could have wished for in a father. Well, almost everything. She knew he wasn't going to stay.

Still, now Jimmy had a full set of parents. No one could ever take that away from him again.

"Let's go out to eat," Ken suggested as the shadows lengthened. "How about that seafood place from the other night?"

Jimmy looked surprised when he realized Ken was including him. He agreed to go along without enthusiasm, but without any particular resentment, either. Shawnee picked out a dress she knew would enhance her figure and stopped to look at herself in the mirror. What she saw was unfamiliar. Slinky silver-blue silk held up by tiny spaghetti straps, the entire outfit showing off her shape and making her feel sexy. It had been a long, long time since she'd tried to look good for a man. She'd almost forgotten how to make the most of what she had, almost forgotten how to attract.

But... "Nah," she said, laughing at herself as she looked in the mirror. She would never forget that. "Once you learn," she told herself with a grin, "you never forget it. It's in the blood."

Ken's look when she came out made the effort worthwhile. His hot gaze set off a sizzle just beneath the surface. It was really fun having a man around.

Arriving at the restaurant, they had barely sat down and ordered drinks when Reggie and Lani showed up. Reggie was attired in his usual loud but well-cut shirt, and Lani actually had on a dress. With a little bit of neckline and no baseball cap, she looked downright pretty.

"Hey, you guys," Reggie called out as he spotted where they were sitting. "I thought we might find you here."

"Good thinking." Ken rose to greet them, and Shawnee smiled.

"Join us," she said. "We haven't ordered yet."

Reggie turned to Ken. "Is that okay with you?" He didn't wait for an answer. "Wow," he said, looking from Ken to Jimmy and back again. "Wow. That's incredible. Talk about your chips off the old block."

Ken took his comments with a laugh, but Shawnee could see that Jimmy was uncomfortable. He wasn't used to having a father to cart around, but even worse, he wasn't used to all the things about his mother this new man in the family brought to light. She tried making eye contact with Ken, but he was caught up in Reggie's line of blarney and didn't notice. Still, Ken had sense. She was pretty sure she could count on him to be sensitive to Jimmy's low threshold of embarrassment.

"I figured you'd probably been thinking over my project all day," Reggie was saying. "Intriguing, isn't it? I thought you might want to talk money so I'd better show up." His face was alive with eager anticipation.

Ken laughed and slapped him on the back. "You're quite a salesman, Reggie," he said. "Sit down. We'll get you two something to drink."

Reggie sat down beside Ken and Lani hesitated, looking at Jimmy, her face expectant. He caught sight of her and did a double take, as though he'd suddenly realized he knew her. "Hey, Lani," he said very casually. "Howzit goin'?"

"Hi, Jimmy." Her cheeks reddened and she looked at the empty seat next to him, then looked away quickly and came around the table to sit by Reggie instead.

Shawnee saw the entire exchange. Poor baby, she moaned silently. Don't fall in love with my Jimmy. There are already too many girls in love with him, and I'm very much afraid you're just not his type.

But out loud she only said, "Sit down, Lani. It's good to see you again."

The girl slipped into a chair and nodded to her, then sat back, looking very ill at ease in her outfit.

Ill at ease, Shawnee thought with a smile, but definitely lovely. She couldn't help but wonder if the dress was because of the dinner out, or purely for Jimmy's sake—Jimmy, who wasn't even looking her way. He was following the conversation between Reggie and his father and Shawnee wished she could read his thoughts from his expression.

"Well, come on," Ken was saying, obviously enjoying Reggie's line of bull. "What happened today? Did you go out?"

"We went out and checked out the site," Reggie answered, looking about the table grandly as though to command an audience. "Things look good, real good. Our biggest problem right now is finding rubber rafts."

"Rubber rafts?" Jimmy asked, leaning forward. He had only the sketchiest idea of what they were talking about. "What for?"

Quickly, Reggie explained the project in some detail, then went back to fretting about the rafts.

"I know a guy who's got a whole warehouse full of rubber rafts over Kailua way," Jimmy said, glancing at Ken, then back at Reggie. "I bet he'd sell you a couple."

Reggie's face lit up. He'd been wanting to get Jimmy involved and here was a chance. "Listen, what are you doing tomorrow morning?" he asked Jimmy. "You want to help me go over and get a few?"

Jimmy hesitated, looking at Ken. It was evident he still wanted to keep things at an arm's length for now. "I've got some stuff I've got to do tomorrow," he said evasively. "I'll give you the address."

"Okay," Reggie said. "How about you, Ken? Want to get involved?" His face was alight with expectation. Clearly, when Reggie talked about getting "involved," he meant body and soul.

Ken looked at Shawnee. She wasn't sure if he was asking for permission or advice or what, but she frowned slightly and shook her head. Ken laughed and winked at her. He obviously had a mind of his own. "Sure, Reggie," he said. "I'd like to see what's going on."

"You won't regret it," Reggie chortled, delighted. "This is just going to be great, wait and see."

Shawnee sighed. What was the use? Reggie was like that. He had a knack for drawing people into his plans. He also had a knack for choosing plans that were sure to bomb. It looked like Ken was going to have to learn the hard way.

She'd promised him some money earlier that day, hoping he would stop badgering Ken for financial backing. But obviously it hadn't been enough. Well, Ken was on his own. He was a big boy, after all.

"Did you see any mermaids today?" she asked with a twinkle in her eyes.

"No," Reggie said, somewhat taken aback. "You don't see mermaids like that, right out in the open. They know you're there and they hide."

Shawnee's eyes widened and she nodded with mock wisdom. "So I've always heard. And you think they're not going to notice the rubber rafts?" she pointed out.

Reggie was getting a bit impatient with her lack of faith. "No. I told you, we're going to camouflage them with moss and branches and stuff."

She vaguely remembered having been told all this before, but it must have been at a time when she wasn't paying much attention. Rubber rafts covered with foliage—this was going to be something to see.

Shawnee met Ken's gaze and got him to smile back. Reggie was bending his ear and he was being so nice to him. She loved him for it. There was a gentle happiness surrounding her for the moment. She watched as Reggie talked, turning to Lani now and then for backup. But Lani's sideways glances were all focused on Jimmy. Jimmy—who barely knew she existed.

But Shawnee couldn't let little things like that bother her right now. She was too happy. They'd ordered the food and the music was playing and everything seemed to be circling her world as though she were in the middle of a great big carousel. Bright lights were flashing and things were moving, but there was a sense of peace here in the middle, a peace brought on by the man sitting across the table from her. She was so glad he had come back. How could she ever have tried to evade him?

He rose, excusing himself to make a telephone call, and she watched him walk away, admiring the set of his shoulders, his tall, lean looks. As she looked on, one female head after another turned, gazes following his progression. Laughter bubbled up her throat at the sight.

"Mine," she whispered to herself. "Hands off, ladies."

Filled with her own brand of happiness, she wanted the same for everyone around her. The band was playing. People were dancing. Suddenly she had an idea. Leaning forward, she gestured for Jimmy to listen. "Dance with Lani," she whispered to him.

His reaction was surprise. "What? Why?"

She frowned at him. "Come on, Jimmy," she whispered to him. "She needs someone to ask her to dance."

Despite her soft voice, Lani picked up on what was going on and saw the reluctance on Jimmy's face, even though he tried to hide it as he got up and began to come around the table. Leaning over quickly, she said something to Reggie, and when Jimmy got to her, she turned him down with a quick shake of her head.

"Sorry, Jimmy, but Reggie's just asked me to dance with him. Haven't you, Reg?"

Reggie looked a little puzzled, but amenable. "Sure thing, Lani," he said, shoving back his chair. "Let's go."

Lani's dark eyes were defiant as she looked up at Jimmy. "Excuse me," she said tartly as she pushed past him to get to where Reggie was waiting to escort her to the floor.

Jimmy turned and gave his mother a baleful look before he sank once again into the vacant chair beside her. "I tried," he said.

She patted his knee, laughing. "You did try, and I thank you for it." Her smile faded as she tried to read what was going on behind his eyes. "Are you all right?" she asked him softly.

He looked up at her, startled. "Sure. Why wouldn't I be?"

"You know very well why. You've had to accept a lot of readjustments. I'm...I'm just sorry you have to go through this, Jimmy. It's my fault and..."

He grabbed her hand and squeezed very tightly. "It's not your fault," he said, his voice husky. "I know it's not your fault. And don't worry about me. I'm okay."

He wasn't, though, not really. She could see it in his eyes. What Ken had told him had gone a long way toward bringing him back to normal. But he wasn't all the way back. Maybe he never would be.

But she sat silently beside him, holding his hand, and hoping for the best. She had an irrational certainty that Ken would fix things. He should never have begun taking care of her the way he had the day before. Now that she knew how good it felt, she was going to have trouble letting it go.

Nine

Ken was on the phone, talking to Karen and thinking about the two worlds he was torn between instead of listening to her words. The public telephone was placed near the bar and from where he stood, he could see Shawnee and Jimmy talking earnestly together at the table. On the telephone was Karen, trying to keep her temper, trying to understand why he would be late—again. He'd managed to call her periodically over the past twenty-four hours, but she didn't understand what was going on. He hadn't told her about Jimmy yet. She didn't even really know about Shawnee, though she suspected his absences had something to do with a woman. He was going to have to tell her all about everything tonight.

Funny. A few hours before he'd been tempted to run away from Shawnee and his son and all the difficulties involved in his relationship with them. Now he was thinking of running away again, but this time it was Karen and his life on

the mainland he wished he could avoid. And it was Shawnee he wanted to run to. Shawnee and Jimmy.

In his hand he held the representation of his real life on
the mainland. Meanwhile his gaze was full of the two at the
table and they were drawing him, pulling him in. The light
was shining in Shawnee's hair. She was wearing a blue dress
that clung in all the best possible places to cling, and just
looking at her made his blood run a little hotter.

"Ken? Ken?"

"Hmm?"

"Ken, are you listening to me?"

"Sorry, Karen. It's ... it's noisy in here with the band
playing. What were you saying?"

"Oh, Ken, I just don't understand what's wrong. We were
having such a nice vacation until you ran into that friend of
yours ... What's her name again? Sara?"

"Shawnee." He cleared his throat. "Listen, Karen, I
won't be late tonight. I've got something I have to explain
to you. Get the kids to sleep and I'll drop by your room
about ten. Okay?"

There was silence on the other end for a moment.
"Okay," she said at last, and the tremor of fear in her voice
made him wince and filled him with remorse. "I'll wait for
you."

"Good. I'll see you later."

"Ken?"

"What?"

"Nothing. Only ... be careful. Goodbye."

He hung up and swore softly. Karen always managed to
make him feel so damned guilty. He had to remember,
though, every time this happened, just what she was. She
was a part of his real life, along with his mainland law
practice and other commitments. Real life was something
you did because it was a part of you. This, what he was doing here, with Shawnee and Jimmy, this was the part of his

life that was the dream. And dreams were something you had to wake up from.

Shawnee looked up as he returned to the table. He saw the way her eyes lit up when she caught sight of him, and something swelled deep inside. Lord, but it was going to be hard to leave her again.

"May I have this dance?" he asked with a deep bow.

She laughed softly and rose to curl into his arms. "You may have any dance you choose," she told him, her voice holding just a hint of the sensuality that quickened his pulse.

Her body felt light and graceful against his, as though she'd been made especially to fit his specifications. She flowed against him, her scent rising to fill his head. He had to hold his breath for a moment to force back the surge of desire that threatened. This was getting ridiculous. He had to get his mind on other things.

But it was impossible. With her so close, and the memory of the love they'd made that day so vivid in his mind, he couldn't get her out of his head. He blinked away the image of her naked on the bed and found it immediately replaced by the picture she'd made in that electric blue swimsuit. Push that away and he began to imagine how her breasts looked right now with the silky fabric she wore clinging to them. His mind and body weren't listening to reason tonight. He swore a vicious oath and she reared back, stunned.

"What on earth . . . ?"

"Nothing," he told her quickly, pressing her head back down against his chest with his hand and keeping his breathing as even as he could. "Don't pay any attention to me. Pretend I'm not here."

She chuckled softly, snuggling against him. "Not here?" she repeated. "Then where shall I pretend you are?"

"In a cold shower somewhere," he said through gritted teeth. "Preferably at the North Pole."

"Ken . . ."

"Keep your head down," he ordered again, putting one hand at the back of her neck. "Believe me, this is hurting me more than it will ever hurt you."

Before she could protest again, Reggie's voice cut in, and Ken had to let her go.

"Hey, Shawnee, look who's here."

Ken turned as he released her and found Reggie coming across the dance floor, weaving in and out among the dancing couples, towing behind him a handsome dark man dressed only in a sort of elaborate loincloth, his exaggeratedly muscular body oiled and shining.

Shawnee's face broke into a welcoming smile the moment she spotted him. "Raki!" she cried, and started toward him as though for a hug.

"Uh-uh," he warned, stepping back to avoid her embrace. "I'm all greased up for my act. We go on in half an hour. Better not touch." He grinned at her, his dark eyes flashing. "Not until after the show, anyway. Then you can do all the touching you want." He wiggled his eyebrows suggestively at her and she laughed. "Hey, Shawnee, lookin' good in that dress," he said, eyeing her appreciatively, his impertinent gaze running up and down and taking it all in.

She laughed and turned. "Ken, this is Raki," she said, drawing him into the circle. "He and his brothers belong to a troupe of dancing Samoans. They are good friends of my brother, Mitchell."

"We are fire dancers," Raki said proudly, flexing. "We travel from resort area to resort area during the season. We're doing good these days, Shawnee. Not like the old days when you used to put us up at your place. We got bookings through Christmas already."

"That's great. And we're going to get to see you dance tonight?"

"If you stay for the show." Raki winked at her. "I've got some new moves, Shawnee. You gotta see 'em. I want to know if they turn you on."

Ken's original impulse to like the gregarious Samoan was evaporating rapidly and he was just about to say something to let him know it when Reggie broke in again and made things even worse.

"Listen, Shawnee, the reason I brought Raki out here to see you was because he told me he and the boys just got kicked out of their hotel."

"They couldn't take our drums," Raki told her solemnly. "Can you believe it? We were only playing softly. You know how we do. They said we were disturbing the peace." He shook his head. "I think they might have let us go with just a warning, except they saw Kane cooking a lizard on a little fire in his room." He sighed heavily. "As if he didn't know how to control a little fire like that. He's been cooking all his life and he never burned down a building yet." He hesitated, remembering. "Well, there was that little house on Maui. But it was scheduled for demolition, anyway. So there was no real harm."

"So the boys need someplace to stay," Reggie continued helpfully. "And I remembered how you used to put them up and I said, 'Hey, let's go see Shawnee. I know she has room.'"

"Why sure, Raki," Shawnee said quickly, glancing at Ken and then away. "I'd love to have you all over at my place—"

"If only she could," Ken interrupted firmly, his hand on her shoulder. "It's too bad, but that's going to be impossible."

"Impossible?" Shawnee stared at him blankly. "Why?"

"Impossible?" Reggie echoed, bewildered. "Why?"

"Why?" Ken looked from one puzzled face to the other. The real answer was as plain as day. With a gaggle of fire-breathing Samoans around, he would never get a minute alone with Shawnee. Besides, this Raki guy was just a hair too familiar. There was no way he was going to let him sleep anywhere near her.

"Why?" he repeated, suddenly realizing he was full of real reasons he couldn't reveal and yet didn't have a clue as to what he could say to cover for himself.

"Yes," Reggie said suspiciously. "Why?"

"Because she's getting the interior of her house coated with fiberglass," he said off the top of his head. "They started spraying today. It's going to take them a week to finish. There are shards of fiberglass everywhere. Shawnee can't go into her own house without putting on protective gear and a gas mask. There's no way she can have company."

Reggie looked thunderstruck. "Fiberglass coating inside your house?" he said. "Wow. What's that like?"

Shawnee was laughing quietly, trying to avoid meeting anyone's eyes for fear of bursting out with it.

"What's it like, Shawnee?" her cousin asked again.

"Weird," she said in a choked voice, glancing at Ken and suppressing her laughter. "Very, very weird."

"It's going to be invisible," Ken announced, warming to his topic. "You won't be able to see a thing. But everything in the house—the carpet, the walls, the furniture, the bookcases—everything will be protected by the fiberglass coating. Things will last forever."

Reggie was still confused. "This must be something new, huh? I wonder if it's an industry I ought to look into. I mean, if you got into the bottom floor on a thing like this..."

"You've got enough to handle with your documentary project," Shawnee reminded him quickly. "Why don't you concentrate on that for a while?"

"You're probably right." Reggie sighed. "Come on, Raki. Let's go see if Florence, the head waitress, can give you guys a place to stay. She lives in a commune down by the beach. You'd love it...."

Ken pulled Shawnee back into his arms and they danced while she laughed. "That was very bad," she told him, pretending to scold. "You mustn't think you can make my decisions for me that way."

"Of course not," he said smoothly. "You could have called me a liar at any time. That was your prerogative."

She shook her head, loving him, loving his possessiveness. "Poor Reggie—" she began.

"Poor Reggie, nothing," he broke in. "He was trying to fix you up with that guy."

"That's a bit extreme. He was just trying to make everyone happy. He's such a dear."

Ken grunted. "Dear or not, I'll kill him next time he tries that," he muttered.

"No, you won't. You'd be killing off your own partner." She sobered. "Speaking of which—you know, this is crazy, Ken. I've been meaning to talk to you about it. You're not really going to invest in Reggie's scheme, are you?"

"Why not?" He leaned closer and discretely nuzzled her neck. "I like Reggie. Or I did before he started tossing Samoans in your lap. And I've got the money."

"Have you also got a soft spot in your head?" she demanded tartly. "Reggie is a darling, but his schemes always fall through. He dreams big, but the follow-through is usually a little off key."

He grinned, curling his hand around hers. "How can you say that, Shawnee?" he teased. "Mermaids lurking inside the reef, hiding from tourists but coming out to play when only friendly *kamaainas* are around...."

"Hey." She laughed softly. "You're even beginning to speak my language."

"Sure," he said, drawing her closer. "Everything about you enchants me, Shawnee. Haven't you figured that out yet?"

Warmth poured through her soul like buttered rum and she let it, savoring the feeling, savoring the love she was so starved for. But in the back of her mind, reality lingered, keeping her from going overboard. She could bask in the glow of his affection for now, but she knew better than to let it go to her head. You could count on only what you put into this old world. You could never count on anyone else. That was something she was never going to let herself forget.

They danced until the music stopped, then finally went back to the table with the others, but there seemed to be someone missing.

"Where did Jimmy go?" Shawnee asked as they sat down.

Lani looked up, her face void of any expression. "He said he had to go see his girlfriend about something. He said to tell you he'd be home late tonight."

Shawnee and Ken exchanged glances and a lot of the humor went out of the evening. Jimmy was still upset. That much was clear.

"He just needs some time alone," Ken murmured to her. "Don't worry."

She nodded and tried to smile, but it was an effort. Jimmy taking comfort in the arms of his girlfriend could have nightmare ramifications. Be careful, Jimmy, she said silently to herself. Oh, please be careful, darling.

The next day started out raining and drizzly, but Shawnee's spirits were high, anyway. Jimmy hadn't stayed out late the night before, after all, and when he'd come home, he'd been downright normal. She had a lot of hope at the moment, and she sang as she cooked breakfast.

Jimmy came out, looking sleepy and disheveled. "What are you making all that racket for?" he demanded in a grumpy voice. "It's too early."

Her smile was spontaneous. "I can't help it. I just feel like singing."

He stared at her, his face shadowed. "You're really happy, aren't you, Mom?" he said softly.

Looking up, she smiled again. "Sure. I'm always happy."

"No." He shook his head. "Not like this." He frowned, trying to get it right. "There's like . . . this light shining inside you or something."

A light shining inside her. That was exactly how she felt. "I can't imagine why that should be," she said lightly, though she knew very well.

He kept staring for a moment longer, then gave up. "Yeah, right," he grumbled, stomping off to the bedroom. "Pipe down out here, okay?"

She turned and watched him go. It was Ken, of course. Ken was filling her with happiness. And even knowing it couldn't last wasn't diminishing it one bit. "You're a complete idiot, Shawnee Caine," she told herself. "If you had any sense at all, you'd be crying like a baby."

But she had no sense, so she went back to singing, just keeping it low so as not to wake sleeping dogs. When Jimmy came out a bit later, all showered and fresh-looking, he didn't mince words.

"Do you love him?" he asked her, his voice strained but his chin firm.

She caught her breath and turned to look him in the face. "I did," she said softly.

Jimmy's eyes were huge. He was waiting for more, and suddenly she thought she knew exactly what he needed.

"We both loved each other," she told him simply. "We were much too young and very foolish. We were both hurting. And when we found each other, it was as though we'd been given a gift.''

Jimmy's eyes didn't waver, but he didn't say a word. Stepping forward, she touched his cheek and smiled.

''We went too far, of course,'' she added. ''And you've had to pay the price. I'm sorry about that. It wasn't fair to you.''

Jimmy swallowed. ''Did he...? Did he...?'' He couldn't seem to get it out, but she thought she knew what he had to know.

''Jimmy, your father and I made love once, next to a waterfall, at a time when we were so in love, we were blinded by it. He didn't force me. I didn't trick him. It was beautiful and right for the moment, even though it was crazy and dangerous. And when I realized I was pregnant, I was scared, but even more than that, I was so happy to know I was having Ken's child. You were a surprise, my darling, but you were always a joy.''

He stared at her for a moment, then nodded silently and left the room. She watched him go, her eyes full of tears, and prayed that he would someday understand.

The sun came out later, drying up all the little puddles. Jimmy went with her to the café and helped her work the lunch shift. They were just cleaning up with only a couple of customers left, when Ken arrived.

''Know any place a man can get a decent meal around here?'' he asked her in his best imitation of a forties film star.

''I don't know. That depends on what you mean by decent,'' she vamped back, batting her eyelashes. ''What do you think, big boy?''

He grabbed her around the waist and bent her backward over his arm. ''I'm thinking I'll settle for indecent,'' he said gruffly. ''How about it, Toots? You know how to show a fella a good time?''

"I know how to show a fella the door," she protested, laughing as he let her back up. She glanced around the place and saw her waitresses giggling at the entrance to the kitchen. "Let me go, Ken," she remonstrated out the side of her mouth. "We can't act like this here."

He shrugged. "It's your place, isn't it? You ought to be able to act any way you want." But he let her go and she smoothed her apron and her hair.

"Jimmy's here," she told him, scanning the hallway guiltily. "I really don't think we should do this in front of him."

He wanted to say something, challenge her on this, but he swallowed his words and bit his tongue. After all, she knew best where Jimmy was concerned. At least for now. And he didn't want to do anything to ruin the tentative connections he was making with the boy. That wouldn't be worth it.

He let Shawnee make him a hamburger and milk shake, and she sat with him while he ate. When Jimmy came out with a load of fresh silverware, he hailed him.

"Hey, Jimmy. How about coming out to Hamakua Point and giving us a hand?"

Jimmy's eyes were shadowed by something uneasy. He stuck his hands in his pockets. "What for?" he asked, almost sounding suspicious.

"Well, we got the rafts, and they're inflated and ready to go. Lani and Reggie have been decorating them with every piece of flotsam and jetsam they can find. They look like two mini garbage barges to me, but they seem pleased with them. The problem is, now that we have them ready to go, we realize there's no way to move them through the water without paddles or motors. Either one is going to scare off the mermaids."

"But, Ken..." Shawnee stared at him. Surely he wasn't falling for this line of Reggie's. "Wait a minute. How can mermaids be scared off when there *are* no mermaids?"

"Huh?" He blinked at her as though he didn't understand. "Listen, lady, if there were no mermaids, what would we be doing out there?"

She nodded, smiling blandly. "Exactly my point."

Turning away from her in disgust, he appealed to Jimmy. "Your mother is a skeptic, obviously not to be trusted. But you'll help us, won't you?"

Jimmy couldn't help it. There was a twinkle in his eyes and it looked as though he'd almost laughed. He hesitated, made as if to run for it, then turned back. "What do you need me to do?" he asked.

"Swim."

"Huh?"

"We've got two rafts to move. You take one, I'll take the other. We'll lead them with ropes."

He'd appealed to Jimmy's sense of curiosity. Shawnee watched as indecision gave way to reluctant acceptance in his eyes. He couldn't resist going out to see what was really going on.

"Okay," Jimmy said, loath but pliable. "I guess I could help for a little while."

And that was how it all began. For the next two days, Jimmy was glued to Ken's side. They went out at the crack of dawn and floated around in the silly-looking rafts until dusk. Shawnee took them a midmorning snack and lunch at noon, and then in the afternoon she came and sat in the grass and watched as they scooted up and down the coastline.

"No luck, huh?" she said as they disembarked for the evening, tired and hungry.

"They're out there," Reggie insisted, his eyes just a little wild. "I can sense them out there." Turning, he stared back at the inky sea. "If I could just find a way to talk to them," he muttered mostly to himself. "If I could just explain . . ."

Shawnee looked at Ken questioningly. "Is he all right?" she whispered, pulling him out of earshot. "Do you think we should get help for him?"

"For Reggie?" Ken glanced at the man and shook his head. "Are you kidding?" he said with quick humor. "He's our leader, our prophet. He sees things the rest of us can't."

"I know," she said evenly. "That's just the problem." But it was a problem she soon forgot as Ken swept her into his arms and kissed her soundly.

"Take me home," he groaned. "My joints are rusting."

Jimmy appeared out of nowhere and Shawnee struggled in Ken's arms, trying to get free. But Ken's arms tightened, holding her.

"We're his parents, Shawnee," he whispered. "He's got to get used to how we feel about each other."

She relaxed a little, turning so that Ken's arm was around her but not holding her in an embrace, and she forced herself to look into Jimmy's eyes to see what he was thinking.

To her surprise, there was not a clue. He came walking up to them as though this were something he'd seen them doing all his life, his eyes full of excitement for the job at hand.

"We got some great footage," he announced, waving the camera at her. "This underwater rig Reggie got hold of is fantastic. Wait'll you see the reef life on this tape. I got a perfect shot of Reggie stepping on a sea slug."

"Jacques Cousteau would be proud," she admitted. "But that's still not mermaids."

He looked at his mother as though he'd just realized she was nuts. "Mother," he said slowly, "there are no such things as mermaids. Face it." And he stomped off with the camera.

Shawnee turned, her mouth open in silent outrage, until she caught Ken's eye and they both burst into laughter.

That night they lit a fire at the beach and roasted marshmallows on sticks and sang old songs. And for the very first time, Shawnee could almost pretend they were a real family together.

Shawnee was humming again as she finished wiping down the tables the next afternoon. She was always humming lately. But when she turned and saw the blond woman standing in the doorway with a child held by either hand, the humming died in her throat. Somehow she knew right away who this was. Going forward, she held out her hand.

"It's Karen, isn't it?" she said.

Karen blinked at her. Her face was pretty but a bit careworn. "Are you Shawnee?" she asked sweetly. "I thought I should come over and meet you. I think we should get to know each other, don't you?"

"Certainly. Won't you come on in?" Dread was building a fortress in her stomach, but she wasn't going to let it show. She glanced at the children. "Why don't I have one of my waitresses set the children up with ice cream at the far table? Then we can have some time alone to talk."

"That would be fine." Karen went down on one knee and spoke to the boy and girl, each dressed as though they were about to take part in a fashion shoot, telling them she would only be a moment. They went off happily, quiet and well-behaved. Shawnee had to give it to Karen. She seemed to be a very good mother.

She also didn't waste any time in getting to the point.

"I met your son today," she said as soon as they were seated, facing one another in a remote booth. "Ken brought him by to introduce him to me. He's a beautiful boy. He looks so much like Ken."

So she knew all about it. That was a relief, in a way. Shawnee hadn't relished the prospect of trying to dance around the subject, not knowing how much Ken had told her.

"Thank you," she said simply. "I think so, too."

"I'm sure he's a lot like his father."

"In some ways. But he's pretty much his own person most of the time."

"Of course."

There was a long silence that seemed horribly awkward until Shawnee realized Karen was mentally composing herself for the presentation she was about to make. Her hands were folded quietly before her. Two tiny red spots sat on her cheekbones. This wasn't easy for her, but obviously she felt it was something that had to be done.

When she finally spoke, she dropped a bombshell in Shawnee's lap. "Ken was the backbone of my marriage, you know," she said calmly. "I couldn't have survived without him."

Shawnee felt as though she'd just been nudged with a cattle prod. "What?" she said hoarsely.

"It's true." Karen nodded her blond head. "Gary—my husband—was a wonderful man in many ways, but he loved his work more than he loved me or the children. He was never home, never there whenever there was a crisis. Ken was the one I always leaned on." She gazed levelly into Shawnee's eyes. "Ken was always there when I needed him. Always."

Why was there suddenly a lump in her throat? "I see," she managed to force out around it. But she really didn't see at all. Or maybe it was that she didn't *want* to see. She pulled on the neckline of her blouse, wondering why it seemed to have gotten so hot in the café so quickly.

"Did Ken tell you about how Gary died in January? He was running for a plane and was hit by a taxicab. He was always running for something . . . a meeting, a lecture, an opening of one of his businesses, the final stages of a deal. Always in a hurry to get to the next place. That was the way we got married, too, in a big hurry. And then, once he was sure this was a real situation, he left to go on to the next challenge." Her eyes closed for a moment, then she smiled sadly. "Oh, we didn't separate or anything like that. But he was so involved with his work, sometimes he even slept in his office. He was more at home at work than he was in the house I was keeping for him."

Shawnee shook her head and murmured something meant to be comforting, but what could she say? She sympathized with Karen. But what did all this have to do with her?

No, that was silly. It had everything to do with her and she knew it. The woman was trying to explain to her why she couldn't have Ken. Ken was already spoken for. Ken was busy. Leave him alone. That was the very clear message here.

"My children—Kimmy and Jeff—have spent more Sunday afternoons with Ken than they ever spent with their own father. They love him." The woman's hand shot out suddenly and grabbed Shawnee's wrist. "They need him," she said fervently. "And that is something I know you can understand. After all, your son didn't have him while he was growing up, did he? And I'm sure you wished, all these years, that Jimmy's father was here to help raise him—to give him an example to follow—to give him the love and self-esteem he needed so badly."

To Shawnee's horror, tears were pricking at the back of her eyes, as though the woman had turned on just the right switch at just the right time. Anger swept through her. She refused to be manipulated like this.

"We did just fine without Ken," she said defensively, then immediately regretted it.

"Of course, you did." Karen patted her hand condescendingly. "Of course, you did. He seems to be a fine young man." Her face took on a tragic air. "But I think you must be a stronger woman than I am, Shawnee. When I look at my two little ones and think of trying to raise them

all alone..." Her voice broke and she drew her hand back
to reach for a handkerchief.

Shawnee averted her eyes so as not to show the scorn she
felt. The woman was playing this for all it was worth.

"Karen," she said evenly. "I know it must be hard to lose
your husband. And I'm sorry for all that you will undoubt-
edly have to go through. But I have a feeling you're asking
something of me. Why don't you come right out and tell me
what it is?"

Karen's hazel eyes hardened. "All right. I appreciate
candor, too. I'll tell you what I want. I want Ken to wrap up
this vacation and fly home with me right away."

Her words were no surprise, but Shawnee felt staggered
by them, anyway. Working hard, she didn't let it show. "I
can't imagine why you're telling me this," she said in a
carefully steadied voice. "Don't you think you ought to take
this up with Ken? After all, it is his decision, not mine."

Karen stared at her for a moment, then sighed. "Let's be
straight all across the board, okay?" she said in a clipped
tone. "You're his old love. He's thrilled that he found you
again. You're exotic and different. He's been working so
hard lately, he needed a diversion, and you've provided
quite an exciting interlude. You're beautiful and exciting to
be with, I'm sure. And then you've got this boy you say is
his...."

Shawnee gasped, eyes widening. "You said yourself you
saw the resemblance," she reminded the woman coldly.

Karen's smile was frigid. "One must be polite. But,
please, I'm not disputing parentage. That's neither here nor
there. You've given him a great gift, in a way. He's en-
thralled by the idea of having a grown son." She leaned
forward, all pleasantries pushed aside. "Bottom line, he's
mine. He's been mine for a long time. He's made certain
commitments to me. We're planning to get married as soon
as a proper amount of time has passed."

Shawnee was shaking inside. Gritting her teeth, she tried very hard not to show it. But Karen's words were weapons meant to slash into her, and they were doing a damn good job of it. She was definitely wounded.

"I need him," Karen went on. "I want him back. My kids need him. And he needs them. Your son is grown. He might have benefitted from having Ken around a few years ago, but he's too old to get much out of it now. At the same time, my kids are crying out with need for him. Be reasonable. Be realistic."

She looked as though she were finished, but had another thought and continued. "And keep this in mind. Ken has a very important law practice that needs him badly. The longer he delays returning, the more things will fall apart. If you love him, it's your place to do what's best for him. Letting his life go to rack and ruin so that he can play 'castaway' in the Pacific would be a tragedy. Think about it." She rose and called to her children.

"Thank you for your time," she said pleasantly as she left. "It's been so nice meeting you."

Shawnee didn't say a thing in return. She got up and walked with Karen to the door, but she didn't speak. She was too stunned to know what to say. Because, much as she hated the woman and hated what she'd said, she knew she had a point. If Shawnee loved Ken, she should do what was best for him. It was the only way.

But she didn't want to! Her mind and her heart were at war. She didn't really care what promises he'd made to anyone else. He'd been hers before he'd ever belonged to anyone else. She wanted him for herself. A fierce determination rose in her. She wasn't going to let this woman come in here and walk away with Ken without a fight.

Ten

She was too shaken to stay at work after Karen's visit. The turmoil of her thoughts and feelings was tearing her apart. Handing out assignments to her manager in a daze, she raced home to an empty house and paced the floor of her living room until she couldn't stand it any longer. Dropping her clothes as she walked across the room, she pulled out her swimsuit and yanked it on, turning to dash out, flying down the steps and running toward the shore, the hot sand burning the soles of her feet.

She swam hard, trying to erase her thoughts. The water was cool and inviting, but it didn't do anything to clear away her troubles. Giving up, she headed for the island. She could at least pretend she was in another world once she got there.

Ken glanced at Karen's set face and made the hard right turn down the cliff face onto the beach and into Shawnee's driveway. He had to be careful. He didn't want to communicate his anger to the children in the back seat. But he was furious with Karen, and she knew it. She'd turned up at the point and disrupted shooting for the day, then told him she'd been to see Shawnee and explained that he had to go home now. Play time was over.

She hadn't put it in exactly those terms, but that was obviously what she meant. He'd piled her and the kids into the car and come chasing back to Shawnee's house to settle things.

But settle what? He pulled the car to a stop in her driveway and sat staring at the house. What did he hope to accomplish here? Did he really think talking things out would result in them all being friends? Did he really think Karen was going to see the way he and Shawnee felt about each other and say, "Oops, sorry. I see the way the land lies now. I'll just go on back home and leave you two alone."

That was hardly likely to happen. Now that he was here, he wasn't sure what he could possibly do that wouldn't just make the situation worse.

Swinging out of the car, he looked down at Karen. "I'll go in first and tell her we're here," he said.

The smile on her face looked painted. "I don't think you'll have much luck," she said coolly. "She seems to be taking a swim."

Turning sharply, he looked out and saw that she was telling the truth. He caught a flash of blue as Shawnee came out of the water and pulled herself up onto a rock on the island. For one long moment, he stared out at her. She was too far away to make out her features, but he knew she was staring back.

His hands went to the buttons on his shirt.

"What are you doing?" Karen cried, alarmed.

He didn't answer. In a moment, his shirt was flapping to the ground and he'd begun on the buttons of his jeans.

Luckily, he was still wearing his swimsuit from the work out on the point.

"You're not going to swim all the way out there!" Karen cried.

He glanced back at her and nodded, his eyes unreadable."Yes," he said as he kicked away his jeans, "I am."

Shawnee watched him coming toward the island. She'd seen him drive up, and she'd seen that Karen was with him. Her heart began to pound and her breath came very quickly. Rising from her rock, she turned and went into the interior of the little island, in where a small lagoon lay hidden among the banyan trees. Purple orchids were scattered along the banks, and the scent of plumeria filled the air. Not allowing thought to enter into her mind, she dove deep into the warm water of the lagoon, holding her body straight as an arrow, letting momentum take her as far as it would.

Ken was panting as he pulled himself up onto the banks of the island. He'd seen where Shawnee had gone, but he needed a moment to recuperate from the swim out. Breathing restored to normal, he got up and looked back at the shore. Karen was leaning against the car, watching him, and she had the kids out, playing in the sand. The sunlight reflected off the windshield of the car, blinding him. For just a moment he felt that torn sensation again. Karen was reality, Shawnee was the dream. What was the matter with him? Couldn't he face reality any longer?

Turning abruptly, he made his way through the thick growth in the direction she'd been going when he'd caught sight of her. In just a few moments, he found the lagoon and he stopped, enchanted by the magical scene before him. It was like something out of an old movie. He'd never known such places actually existed.

When Shawnee broke through the skin of the water, surfacing just in front of him, he wasn't surprised. He'd expected to find her. And when she rose, dripping water everywhere, from her hair, from her eyelashes, from her arms, from her breasts, clad in the blue fabric that clung like plastic wrap and emphasized everything beneath it, when she looked at him with an open invitation like he'd never seen before, her full lips half open, her emerald eyes half hidden by her lashes but full of hunger, her arms opening, stretching toward him, he knew why he'd had to come. He knew what she wanted him there for. There was no need to ask any questions.

Stumbling forward, he took her in his arms and held her to him. Her wet face was cool but her mouth was hot. He kissed her deeply, longingly, moving against her lips again and again, and as he kissed her, he felt her hands slide down into his swimsuit and desire surged in him like a flame that wouldn't be stopped until it had consumed everything before it. His mouth still covering hers, he hooked his thumbs beneath the straps of her suit and began to peel the fabric away from her body as she did the same to his, her hands setting off sensations calculated to drive him mad. Her tiny suit felt like smoke in his hands, so thin, so soft, and he tossed it away like he would cast off a spider's web and looked down at what he'd revealed.

Her body was so smooth, so rounded, so completely irresistible, so completely his, that when she first twisted away and dove back into the water, he was stunned for a few seconds, uncomprehending. Diving after her, he chased her through the drowsy water, catching her ankle and yanking her back into his arms. Her body slid against his, feeling at first like a sea animal, and then very much like the most desirable woman he'd ever seen and touched. He wanted to arouse her as she was arousing him, and he teased her nipples, stroked her skin, ran his hand along the inside of her thighs, until she cried out with need for him, and he felt drunk with power. He'd created this urgency in her, and only he could fill her need.

Somehow they had landed on the mossy bank, legs still dangling in the water. She welcomed him with tiny cries and he surged into her as though he were diving into water again. Her legs wrapped around him and her fingers dug into his back, and they clung together while the rhythm played itself out, up and down, around and around, harder, deeper, more...more...

And finally it was over. They lay very still, listening to the hum of insects, the sweet cry of baby birds, the lapping of the water around them.

We're just a part of it all, he thought to himself, trying to get back to sanity like a man trying to reach the surface of the water after a deep, long dive. A part of the natural kingdom. This is something that was meant to be. We can't deny it. And anyway, he thought a bit despairingly, how the hell am I going to live without this, now that I know it's here for me?

Shawnee's thoughts were even darker. She lay as though she couldn't move, with her eyes tightly closed, and hated herself. She couldn't believe she'd done this thing, this awful thing. Here she was, playing island native girl to his conquering explorer—using her body to try to win his love. Was she really such a fool? Or was she merely out of her ever lovin' mind?

"Shawnee..." His large hand swept the hair back away from her face. He wanted to do more, to tell her how he felt. If only he knew how to put it into words. "Shawnee..."

Cringing, she turned away from him. "You'd better get back to Karen," she said stiffly, avoiding his gaze, wishing she could close her eyes and blot out this whole scene. "She'll be wondering what's taking you so long."

He hesitated. What she said was very true. He had to get back. He couldn't leave Karen pacing the beach. But he'd landed in a place where he couldn't see himself doing right by either of these women. No matter what he did, he hurt someone. "I can't leave you here like this," he said.

She made a sound of impatience. "This is my island, Ken. My home. This is where I want to be left."

Sliding down the bank, she sank into the water and began to swim away from him.

He walked along the bank, keeping up with her. "We need to talk," he said. "That's what I brought Karen over for. She told me she went to see you this morning."

"There's nothing to talk about, really," she said, turning on her back and half floating. She couldn't keep herself from looking at him, at his beautiful lean body. She saw the marks her nails had made on his back and her first thought was that she hoped Karen would see them. And then she was ashamed. This was no good. This had to stop. "It's probably time you got yourself back to California," she said curtly. "Don't you think?"

He stopped and looked at her. "We need to talk," he said again. Leaning down, he scooped up his swimsuit and put it on. "But I guess this isn't really a good time to have Karen over, is it? I'll take her to the hotel." He started toward the opening that led to the outside world, turning back at the last moment to add, "I'll be back." And then he was gone.

She wasn't going to cry. No matter what, she wasn't going to cry. Diving back into the water helped. That way, you couldn't see the tears.

Ken didn't come back that night. Jimmy and Reggie and Lani all came tumbling in at dusk, dirty and sunburned and laughing at silly jokes. She fed them all and pretended to laugh along with them, and all the time her heart and soul were full of Ken, waiting for him, watching for him, mourning the fact that he wasn't coming, after all.

Karen had him. Well, that was as it should be. Maybe he would call, just to tell her what was up.

But he didn't call. She saw Reggie and Lani off, and had to listen to Jimmy apologizing on the phone to Misty for another evening not spent with her. She sent him off to bed and read two magazines and heard the clock strike midnight before she would admit it to herself. He wasn't going to call, either.

Was he going to leave without saying goodbye? Her stomach churned at the thought. She knew, she had known from the beginning, that she was going to have to face him leaving, but at least, this time, she ought to get a goodbye.

He didn't show up to take Jimmy to the point, as had become their habit of late. He didn't call before she left for work. When she brought lunch by the project site, he wasn't there. And when she got home, there was nothing on her answering machine.

He's gone, she thought, dying inside. He's already gone.

So she was shocked when he and Jimmy arrived home together that evening.

"Hi," he said, smiling at her with a look that said he might gobble her up if given the chance.

"Hi," she said back, matching her look to his.

"Oh, yuck," Jimmy muttered, leaving them alone. But his grin held not a hint of resentment.

Ken drew her into his arms and kissed her softly, once, twice, and then again. "I missed you," he whispered, rubbing his face against hers.

It was heaven holding him so close. Better than anything. She couldn't answer "I missed you, too," because there was a lump rising in her throat.

"I'm sorry I haven't called or come over. I was busy getting Karen out of here."

She looked up, startled, her heart hammering with sudden adrenaline. "She's gone?"

He nodded. "I sent her back home to California."

What a relief. Still, that didn't tell her much, except that Ken had bought himself a little more time here. "But...what about you?"

He hesitated, looking at her with something of a speculative gleam in his eye. "I'll have to go in about a week, myself."

"A week." She pulled out of his arms and turned away. "One whole week."

"But, Shawnee..." He caught hold of her again. "I've got something I want to talk to you about. A proposition."

"A proposition?" She glared at him, then tried to smile. "Mr. Forrest, I'm not that kind of girl."

"Not that kind of proposition." His face changed. "At least, not exactly." Turning, he led her to the couch and sat down beside her.

"Remember how you told me you would be willing to sell your café and move to Honolulu to find a better situation for Jimmy?"

She nodded, pushing back her hair and wondering if he'd found out some new reason she should be wary of what was going on in her son's life. "Sure. I'm still considering it."

"Well, I've got a better idea." He leaned back and smiled at her. "How about selling the café and coming back to California with me? Jimmy could go to Astor Academy, a great private school just down the street from where I live. And I'd have both of you with me."

Shawnee sat very still, completely stunned. She'd never dreamed he would suggest something like this. All the dream scenarios she'd thought up involved staying here, where she belonged. She didn't know what to think.

"Have you talked to Jimmy about this?"

Ken nodded, watching her. "He's ready to give it a try. How about you?"

How about her? The room was tilting, taking off for space. She could hardly breathe. *What about her?*

"I—I don't know." She clenched her hands together in her lap. "There's so much to consider..."

Some of the light dimmed in his eyes. He'd been hoping she would be a little more enthusiastic. He'd been bursting with it ever since he'd had this idea. It seemed like the perfect answer to him. But maybe she was right. Maybe there was more to consider. "Take your time. You've got a week to make up your mind."

A week. That wasn't long enough. There was so much to think about. But surely Jimmy would back out. He'd been a lot better about Ken over the past couple of days, but he hadn't shown any inclination to run off and live with him. Surely he would balk. After all, he had his girlfriends here, and all his activities.

"Have you asked her yet?"

Suddenly Jimmy was there, grinning at Ken as though there was a special bond between them. Turning to his mother, he couldn't help communicating his excitement.

"California, Mom! And this Astor Academy place sounds cool. Ken says they place ninety percent of their graduates in top colleges."

"You want to go?" Shawnee asked him, a little bewildered, a little thrown off balance by this turn around.

"Yeah, I really do. Ken says he'll get me flying lessons. And don't forget. I've never been to Disneyland."

Leaning down, he gave his mother a peck on the cheek before he took off for the door, whistling. "Gotta go see Misty. Be back later."

She turned to look at Ken, still moving like a sleepwalker. "Is this for real?" she asked softly.

Laughing, he pulled her close. "Yes, it's for real. Shawnee, I really want to do this. I've missed so much of Jimmy's growing up. Let me do this for him while he's still young enough to need me."

A warning signal went off inside her. Jimmy, it blared at her. This was all about Jimmy. This was not about her.

But, of course. That was only natural. He was Jimmy's father and he needed to do something to validate that.

But where did that leave her? What was she to him? Only Jimmy's mother? And where did Karen fit into this picture? Karen had claimed they'd had plans to marry. She had to bring that up, get it out into the open. He had to explain . . .

"You'll think about it?" he asked, tilting her face up so that he could kiss her lips.

"Yes," she told him, kissing him back.

She thought about nothing else for the next two days. The pros and cons were with her every moment. Should she stay or should she go?

This wasn't anything permanent. She understood that from the beginning. He was talking about one year, a year in which Jimmy would get a good education and meet new people and have new experiences, and she would get to be with Ken. Wasn't that what she wanted? And if not that, what?

But she knew what. She knew exactly what. She wanted a husband, not a part-time lover. No, more specifically, she wanted Ken as a husband. No one else. She'd waited all these years, it was no time to stop being picky.

Little by little, it dawned on her. She couldn't go with him. She couldn't give up the business she'd worked all these years to build just for a chance to hang around and pretend he loved her for a year. If it were absolutely necessary for Jimmy's good, she would do it. But Jimmy didn't need her in California. He was going to have his father.

* * *

"Have you decided yet?" he asked as he helped her do dishes one night. Jimmy had left the room and he took the opportunity to nibble at her ear and run a few kisses down her neck. "Are you coming to California?"

Coming to California—note how he put that, she told herself. Not "Are you coming with me?" As though all she needed was him as a ticket to get there and then she was on her own.

"I don't know," she said evasively. "What would I do there?"

"Do?" He looked as though that thought had never entered his mind. "I don't know. Read books. Garden. Wait for me to come home."

She looked at him in comic horror. "Wake up, buddy," she taunted him. "It's the nineties. Women don't do much of that anymore."

He shrugged. "Women don't get the opportunity to do much of that anymore," he amended. "And here I'm giving you a chance to try it. What's so bad about that?"

She hesitated. He actually had a point. But that meant she would be living off him, and that she couldn't accept. Not under these casual circumstances.

"What about Karen?" She finally got up the nerve to ask.

He looked at her blankly, grabbing a handful of silverware to dry. "What about her?" he asked, as though he couldn't see what she would have to do with anything.

"Ken." She licked her lips and tried to think of a way to put this. "You have a relationship with her. She says you've promised certain things..."

"I promised to be around, like any good brother-in-law. That was all."

She hesitated, avoiding his eyes. "She said there was more. She said...that you'd promised to marry her." She looked up quickly to catch his expression.

"What?" Outrage darkened his face. "That's crazy. I've never promised her anything like that." He put down the cloth and took her in his arms. "Listen to me, Shawnee. I've helped Karen for years, because my brother Gary wasn't the best husband in the world, and I felt sorry for her. I don't love her. I never have." He kissed her and smiled. "And she doesn't love me, either. She's just clinging because she's afraid of the future with Gary gone. We've talked it out, she and I. I've told her I would always be around to support her if she needed it, but the rest of my life is my own."

She touched his face with her hand, glad he'd told her this, but not completely reassured. Karen had been pretty adamant. She couldn't see her backing away so easily.

But it was good to know he'd never promised her marriage or anything like it. Of course, Ken wasn't much of a promising guy. He hadn't promised her anything, either, had he?

She thought about things for another two days before she made her decision. When she told him she was ready to discuss things, he felt a cold chill of foreboding. He could tell by her expression that this wasn't going to be what he'd hoped.

They were sitting on the beach, watching the waves hit the reef. It was after midnight. The air was soft and thick and what breeze there was ruffled the palm fronds. She turned and took his hand.

"I want Jimmy to go with you. But I'm going to stay here."

He'd been afraid she was going to say this. In fact, he'd expected it. But her words still turned his heart cold. He looked out at the moonbeams turning the inky sea silver and he picked up a stone near his foot and threw it into the water.

"I thought you wouldn't want him to go without you," he said at last. "What about your commitment to propagating the species?"

"I'm still committed," she said. "But now I don't have to be quite so tunnel-visioned about it. He isn't only depending on me. He's got you."

Ordinarily he would be happy to hear her say something like that, but not now. Now it meant he was going to have to do without her.

Stretching back, he stared at the sky, at the stars like diamonds on black velvet. He'd known from the beginning that there was very little chance he would be able to get her away from her island. She was so much a part of things here. He couldn't imagine the place without her.

When he tried to picture her in San Francisco, the hills and the tall buildings seemed to be closing in on her. Sometimes he thought she would be like a tropical flower on the mainland, beautiful at first, but quick to wilt in the harsher climate. It wasn't what she was meant for. But that didn't mean he was going to give up on trying.

"Why don't you just come for a while?" he said reasonably. "Then, if you don't like it, you can come back."

She shook her head. "No. I've made up my mind. This way you'll have a whole year with Jimmy all to yourself. You deserve to have that."

He turned and looked at her in the moonlight. "I deserve to have you," he said softly.

Reaching out, she touched his hair with quiet affection. She'd thought it all out. There was no point in her going. She would never fit in where he came from. He would be embarrassed by her eventually. How would he explain her to his friends and associates? She would be in the way and Karen would make sure she knew it. In fact, Karen would make sure she was as miserable as possible.

Not that she was afraid of Karen. No, in a fair fight, she was pretty confident all the way around. But what happened between her and Karen really wasn't the point. What Ken really wanted was the point. And if he wasn't ready to come through with a real commitment, she wasn't going to hang around waiting for him to make a decision.

"It's only for a year," she said, knowing a year could be a lifetime. "Then you'll come back. Won't you?"

"Sure," he said.

Maybe, she translated.

And the two of them went back to staring at the sea, as though somewhere out there was an answer to their dilemma, if they would only look long enough.

Eleven

"Shawnee, we need more ice in the punch," Taylor called from the yard. "And could you bring down napkins?"

"Be right down," she called back out the window, waving to her sister-in-law. Turning back, she started scouring the kitchen for napkins.

Jimmy's going-away party was in full swing. All the relatives were here. Practically everyone they knew was here. Her house was crawling with people. There was a pig on a spit in the back, and women were carrying covered dishes in from their cars, putting them out on the long tables she'd set up all over. There was going to be so much food, they wouldn't be able to eat it in a week, even if everyone stayed to help devour it. But that was the way the parties always were on the island.

Lani burst into the kitchen, skidding to a stop before her, dressed in her usual jeans and T-shirt, but minus the baseball cap for once. "We're already out of ice," she informed

Shawnee breathlessly, her eyes sparkling. She seemed to get prettier and prettier all the time. "Jimmy needs the keys to the car. We're going to go for more."

"Here you go." She handed out the keys and smiled as Lani sailed out with them in hand. She hadn't heard Jimmy mention Misty for days now, and that was just fine with her.

Lani was a funny girl. Half the time she showed up on a decrepit motorbike that looked as though it were going to explode on the next hard turn. She talked about being a pilot and didn't seem to care a lot about making herself as pretty as possible like most girls her age did. And that was just what Shawnee liked about her.

"The girl's got character," she muttered to herself.

Lani and Jimmy had been working hard on Reggie's project. Reggie himself seemed to be getting more and more obsessed by it. He was going out at night now, all alone, determined to catch a mermaid unaware. If Shawnee had had more time to think about it, she would have been getting worried about him by now, she knew. His "great ideas" usually didn't last this long or get this involved.

But everything was all wrapped up in Ken at the moment. She had no room to think about much else, except Jimmy, but then, that was part of thinking about Ken.

Everyone had pretty much accepted Ken as Jimmy's father without skipping a beat. There had been a few curious stares, but nothing to write home about. Her relatives were used to convoluted family relationships and they'd taken it all in stride.

Music was playing out in the front. Someone had put together a little group and she could hear guitars and ukuleles. It was about time she got back to the action. But still she hesitated, stopping for a moment to watch two butterflies chase each other across the deck. She would rejoin the party in just a moment. She needed time to make sure she wasn't going to reveal the unshed tears that had been threatening all day.

"Hey." Her brother Mack was climbing the stairs to join her. "Taylor sent me to help you get ice."

"There isn't any." She smiled at her brother, ruffling his hair. Even though this was the person most responsible for the long rift between her and Ken, she didn't blame him. He'd had his own problems. "Jimmy and Lani went to get more."

"I saw them going off together." He grinned down at his sister. "She has a crush on him, you know."

"No kidding. She might as well wear a sign."

He laughed. "That was why I recommended her to Reggie. I knew she would get closer to Jimmy that way."

Shawnee stared at him, incredulous. "Mack Caine, since when did you become a matchmaker?"

"I wouldn't call it that, exactly." He shrugged and looked uncomfortable. "She's such a great girl and you can tell she's not the type a kid like Jimmy would notice at first. So I thought if he got a chance to really know her..."

"Mack." Going up on tiptoes, she gave him a kiss. "You're a special guy, you know that?"

"Aw." He wiped the kiss away, but he grinned at her. "Where are the napkins, then? Taylor said she needed those, too."

She gave him a huge stack of napkins and watched him make his way back to his extremely pregnant wife. Taylor was sitting by the long table, folding silverware into napkins and talking to her young son Ryan when Mack arrived. The first thing he did was put a large hand over her very round belly and the two of them smiled at each other so sweetly, Shawnee felt a wrenching stab of jealousy. To be in love and carrying a child that you both want and anticipate together—that seemed like heaven, a heaven she would probably never know.

It was ironic that Mack, the one who had always been the black sheep of the family, should be the only one out of the four siblings to have settled down to a standard and very happy marriage. What was the matter with the rest of them?

Maybe it was that old pirate legacy. Maybe the heirs of Morgan Caine were doomed to wander restlessly, just as he had in the days of old. Whatever it was, she wished it would go away.

She started back to the party, but before she could join in the general celebration, her other two brothers accosted her.

"Shawnee, beautiful sister of mine," said Mitchell, the baby of the family in name only, his dark, sleekly handsome head with its bright eyes and knowing smile a focal point of feminine interest everywhere he went. "Would you set this grouchy old bear of a brother straight? I'm trying to introduce him to some women, and he's screwing it up. I don't know if he thinks being rude is charming, but it won't work with ladies these days."

"I wasn't rude," Kam told him indignantly. "I was just telling the truth."

"When a woman asks you if you thinks she's too fat to wear a halter-top dress, she's not asking for truth, bro. She's asking for a compliment."

"What good is a compliment going to do her? At least now she'll know not to wear one of those dresses again."

Mitchell and Shawnee both groaned in unison, and Kam looked hurt.

"Okay, I'm sorry I told the truth. Next time, I'll tell her to wear a bikini. Then see how happy she is with the results."

"There are a lot of good-looking women here at this party," Mitchell went on, ignoring Kam's last comment. "If he would just give me half a chance I could fix him up with a hot date in no time."

Kam glowered. "I don't need a woman."

"Oh, Kam, come on. We all need women."

Shawnee sympathized with Mitchell on this one. Kam had always been the good brother, the one who did the responsible thing, and he never did seem to have any luck with romance. She'd always been a big sister to them both, and that came out now.

"Kam, why don't you let Mitch set you up? It's time you started thinking about the future. You might meet someone nice enough to settle down with, and even have a baby. Look how happy Mack and Taylor are."

Mitchell's eyebrows rose. "Settle down and have a baby?" His face twisted in horror. "That's not the kind of girl I'm trying to fix him up with. I want him to have a good time."

Now Shawnee's back was up, too. "Oh, I see. And you can't have a good time with a good girl?"

Mitchell shrugged. "Fact of life. Can't be helped."

Now Kam was laughing and Shawnee was the one who wanted to throttle Mitchell. Raising these two had never been dull, and she missed them, if the truth be known. But they both knew how to get her goat.

Once they'd all calmed down, she remembered that she had an errand for them.

"Would you two go out to Hamakua Point and see if you could drag Reggie in out of the water? Tell him he doesn't have to clean up or anything. I just want him here."

Mitchell sighed and shook his handsome head. "I don't know, Shawn. I don't think he'll come. He's a real goner over that broad."

"'Broad'?" she echoed disapprovingly. "What 'broad'?"

Mitchell gestured. "That mermaid person."

Shawnee felt somewhat left in the dust. She frowned. "What mermaid person?"

"The one he's so obsessed over. The reason he won't come home anymore."

She shook her head despairingly. "But, Mitchell, there *is* no mermaid person."

He spread his hands out. "Tell that to Reggie. I went to the point to see what was going on last night and he told me he knew she was out there because he could hear her voice."

"Her voice?" Shawnee groaned. "And what, pray tell, did she say?"

"He said she was calling his name."

Kam snorted. "Oh, brother. We've got a real problem, don't we? Reggie's in love with the mermaid."

Mitchell grinned. "Hey, when life hands you lemons, make lemonade. He's making a video as it is. This will only add context and drama. I think we've got a real story here, all about dark obsession. Remember that movie about the guy and the big white whale?"

Kam nodded. *"Moby Dick?"*

"That's the one. We can do an epic about Reggie. We can call it . . ."

"How about *Reggie's Sick?*" Kam chimed in.

Mitchell chuckled. "No, how about *The Call of the Sea?*"

"Or maybe, *Three Men and a Mermaid?*" Kam countered with a grin.

"Mermaid and the Beast?"

"No, *Reggie and the Beast.*"

"Make Way for the Mermaid?"

Shawnee hushed them both. "Come on, you guys. This is really serious. If what you say is true, he really thinks she's out there. He thinks he's in love with her. I don't know how to deal with this."

"Neither do I," Mitchell claimed quickly. "All my love affairs have been with living, breathing women. Or so they claimed."

Shawnee and Mitchell turned and looked at Kam, who threw up his hands.

"Hey, don't look at me. I don't know anything about that love stuff. I thought we'd just got through establishing that."

"But you're the lawyer," Shawnee said sensibly. "You can talk him into coming back here with you."

Kam looked like he wanted to argue, but he changed his mind and turned to leave with resignation, grabbing Mitchell by the arm as he did. "Okay, I'll go. But you're coming with me. In case we have to tie him up and drag him here."

She laughed, shaking her head, and went to greet her guests. It was fun seeing so many old friends and relatives, but behind every bit of casual conversation was the knowledge that she was losing the two men she loved more than any others—losing them for a whole year. It made it hard answering questions with a smile on her face, pretending to be happy about how things were going. So it was almost a relief when she found Misty at her elbow.

"Ms. Caine? Hi. Listen, can I talk to you for a minute?"

"Sure, Misty." One look at the girl's face and she could tell this talk was going to have to involve a bit of privacy. "Come on up to the house. I've got to get something from the kitchen, anyway. We can talk up there."

The house was empty, but just to be sure, she drew the girl into her bedroom so no one would interrupt them. Misty's pretty eyes were clouded and unhappy, and Shawnee began to feel the cold thread of dread along her spine. Whatever she wanted to say, Shawnee had a feeling she wasn't going to like it.

"Here we go. Sit down beside me on the bed here, and tell me what this is all about."

Misty sat carefully on the edge of the bed and looked at Shawnee with eyes swimming in tears. "I—I just don't know what to do. I'm so scared."

Despite how she felt about the girl, she couldn't help but respond to a human being in need. Reaching out, she put an arm around the girl's shoulders, and at the same time, she silently prayed, Let this all be about not wanting to see Jimmy go. Let that be all there is to it. Please. Aloud, she said, "What is it, Misty? What's wrong?"

"I'm . . . I'm pregnant."

Even though she'd been half expecting to hear this once she'd seen the girl's face, the bottom fell out of Shawnee's world with a suddenness that took her breath away. "Oh, no," she whispered, closing her eyes for a moment. "Oh, no."

"I haven't told Jimmy yet. I don't know what to do, because I know he's looking forward to going to this fancy school in California and I don't want to ruin his life. But. . . I have to think about me, you know? And . . . and the baby. And I don't know what to do."

Shawnee's arm tightened around the girl. After her brief moment of horror, she was in control again. "Don't worry, Misty," she said crisply. "We're not going to leave you all alone to make your decisions." She took a deep breath. "Have you told your parents?"

"My parents are divorced and I haven't seen my father for a long time. But my mom . . . I can't tell her. She'll probably kick me out when she finds out." The huge eyes filled with tears again. "I don't know what to do."

"Misty, it's all right. We'll go over your options. We'll look at all the facts and give you the information you need to make the right decision." What was she saying? She hardly knew. She was just talking, throwing out words that didn't have any real meaning to her. Misty was pregnant. How could history be repeating itself this way? Didn't anyone ever learn anything?

"I guess you know how I feel, huh?" Misty said, looking up at her. "I mean, isn't this what happened to you? When you had Jimmy, I mean."

Shawnee stared at her, startled. Of course, Misty knew about Jimmy's background. Just about everybody knew by now. But something in her didn't want to be compared to what was going on here. And seconds after she had that thought, she pushed it away. That was hardly fair. Misty was pretty much in the same position she'd found herself in. Only Misty still had the option of telling the boy who'd fathered her child what was going on.

Well, what now? Should she call Jimmy in and confront him? Should she get Ken involved?

Of course, she should get Ken involved. He was always telling her she wasn't alone any longer, that he wanted to help share her burden of parenthood. And here was a prime problem. She would be only too glad to share the responsibility for any decisions on this one.

"You wait here," she said, sliding off the bed. "I'm going to get Jimmy's father."

Misty's eyes widened. "Are you sure? He won't yell at me, will he?"

"No, I can promise you that. He won't yell at you."

"Okay." She sat back, then seemed to remember something and leaned forward again. "But don't tell Jimmy. Okay? Not yet. I ought to be the one to tell him."

Shawnee nodded and set off to find Ken, her heart heavy, her senses numb. She found him playing volleyball with a group of her younger cousins. He came right away when she signaled.

"What is it?" he asked, panting from the exertion of the game. His hair was falling attractively over his forehead and his face was flushed.

"We have to talk."

She pulled him back behind the hibiscus bushes and gave him the details in a quick, concise outline. He listened with growing outrage, swore and kicked a tree stump.

"Why now?" he said harshly. "This is going to ruin everything. What's the matter with these kids?"

"Ken." She flattened her hand against his chest. "Think. How old were we when this happened to us?"

His eyes darkened and he covered her hand with his own. "Only you were the one whose life was affected," he reminded her. "I got off scot-free."

"At the time." She gave him a dimpled smile that was tinged with sadness. "Now you're going to pay for it."

"Well," he said impatiently, "what do we do? Pay her off? Make them get married? Help her to get an abortion? What?"

"Come and talk to her," Shawnee said after a brief hesitation. "We'll go from there."

He pulled her into the curve of his arm as they walked back to the house, and she settled against his comfort, wondering how she'd gotten along all these years without it.

He managed to hold back his hostility while he talked to Misty. Then he gave Shawnee a sign and they left the girl alone again, promising to be back in a few minutes. He pulled Shawnee into Jimmy's bedroom so that they could discuss things alone.

"What do you think should be done?" she asked bluntly.

He hesitated. "It's just so unfair," he said, swearing softly. "This could ruin Jimmy's life."

She sat down on the bed and stared at the wall. "You're always saying you wished I had found you and told you when I was pregnant," she reminded him quietly. "You're the one who said you would have dropped everything and come to me, who claims college and going to law school would have meant nothing to you if you'd only known."

She glanced over at him. He was staring at her with a faint twist of anger to the set of his mouth, but he didn't stop what she was saying.

"Well, Ken, what do you think now, when it's about your son? Can you bear to see your son's future stunted by a pregnancy that is his fault as much as anyone else's?"

She glanced at him again. His face was twisted in agony.

"You can't blame this on Misty," she reminded him. "Jimmy bears just as much responsibility as she does. Maybe more. He should have used protection." She gazed squarely into his face. "Misty can't be the only one to pay the price. One way or another, Jimmy has to do his share."

Ken nodded slowly, though she could see it pained him to agree with her. "You're right," he said hoarsely. "We've got to get Jimmy into this. He has to do what's right." He sighed and suddenly looked very tired. "I guess the trip to the mainland is off."

Her heart swelled with love for him. She knew how hard it was for him to face this. But his reaction taught her one thing—she would never again doubt that he would have stood by her if she'd been able to find him when she was carrying Jimmy.

"Okay." She rose and stopped to kiss him soundly. "Let's go in and tell Misty she can count on our support."

He caught hold of her hand and let her pull him up. It hurt to think of Jimmy missing out on all the advantages he had been about to give him. But responsibilities had to be attended to. For just a moment he wondered to himself if he were doing this to make up for not being with Shawnee before. Perhaps there was a little of that in his thinking. But, basically, he was just doing it because it was the right thing to do.

They came back into the room to find Misty pacing the floor. As they entered, she turned, looking hopeful.

"Misty, we've talked over your situation," Shawnee told her. "We want you to know that we're here for you. Do you plan to keep the baby?"

Misty looked from one to the other, not answering.

Shawnee frowned. "Maybe we should go over all your options before we call Jimmy into this."

"No!" Misty whirled to stare at her. "I told you I didn't want Jimmy told. Not yet."

"Misty, he'll have to be told," Ken said firmly. "He's the father of the baby. He has rights, too."

Misty looked at them both as though they'd gone crazy. "Jimmy doesn't want any baby, believe me," she said emphatically. "He wants to go to that new school and go to college and all that. This is just going to ruin everything. Poor Jimmy, I..." She glanced at Ken, then at Shawnee, her face sharp and crafty. "You know, I could go to one of those homes where they take care of you while you're waiting to have your baby if you promise to give it up for adoption. I could go and Jimmy would never have to know about it. The only trouble is, those homes cost money. You know what I mean?"

Shawnee shook her head, uncomprehending. "But, Misty, I thought you wanted this baby. I thought you said..."

"Hey, Mom."

The sound of Jimmy's voice ringing out, coming from the entryway, made them all jump.

"Hey, Mom, we're back. We've got the ice. Where do you want it?"

Shawnee sprang up and went to the door of the bedroom. Jimmy was laughing at something Lani had just said. They were both loaded down with bags of ice.

"Jimmy, put that stuff down and come here for a moment," Shawnee said, her voice strained. "We've got something we need to discuss with you."

"No!" Misty was twisting away from the hold Ken had attempted to get on her wrist. "You can't make me stay here," she insisted angrily. "Leave me alone."

Shoving her way past Shawnee, she flew into the living room. Jimmy's face registered surprise at the sight of her.

"Misty? What are you doing here?" he asked.

But Misty wasn't talking. She didn't even acknowledge his existence, pushing past him and throwing Lani a glare before disappearing out the door.

Shawnee turned to look at Ken, who shrugged.

"You got me," he said softly. "Better call Jimmy in and we'll try to get to bottom of this."

"But should *we* tell him?"

He hesitated. "I tell you what, Shawnee. I think we'd better. Ordinarily I'd say it was her place to tell him. But I didn't like the way she was acting. There's something fishy going on."

Shawnee nodded. "I had the same feeling. Let's tell him."

It took a few minutes to orchestrate things, but soon Shawnee had Lani carrying ice out to the backyard, and Jimmy in the bedroom for a talk.

"What was Misty here for?" he asked curiously.

"She came to talk to us," Shawnee said. "She has a problem."

"She's pregnant, Jimmy," Ken told him without waiting for niceties.

Jimmy's first look was astonishment. "Wait a minute. She's pregnant? She told you that?"

Shawnee nodded, hurting for him but steeling herself to do what must be done. "Yes, and since it's as much your responsibility as hers—"

"What did she want?" he broke in. "What did she say?"

Shawnee hesitated. "Well, at first I had the idea that she wanted to have the baby and raise it. She compared herself to me and what I went through when I had you."

Jimmy's green eyes were very cold. "And then?"

"And then she began talking about going to a home for the duration and giving up the baby for adoption."

Jimmy's face looked hard as stone. "Did she ask you for any money?"

"No—"

"No," Ken broke in, "but she was about to when you and Lani interrupted things."

Jimmy shook his head and smiled wryly. "Don't give her any money. It won't do any good."

Shawnee grabbed his arm, alarmed. "Jimmy, what do you mean? You can't just walk away from this."

"Why not?" He rose and kissed his mother on the cheek. "Mom, if Misty is pregnant, she's going to have to go somewhere else to find the father of her baby. It ain't me."

Shawnee gaped at him. "What do you mean?"

"I mean, it can't be me. Misty and I have never slept together." He looked from one parent to the other as they took in this bit of information, both of them stunned. "Wow, you just accepted what she said, didn't you? You really never thought twice." He laughed softly. "Don't you think I'm intelligent enough to learn, Mom? Don't you think I listened to all those lectures you used to give me about respecting women, not having sex until one is prepared to deal with the consequences, and all that? I saw what early sexuality did to your life and I wasn't about to let that happen to mine."

"Jimmy..." She swallowed her words, not really knowing what to say. Far from being a vulnerable child who had to be protected from the rough world around him, she suddenly realized she had raised a son who was stronger than she was at that age. It was quite a revelation.

"No," Jimmy was going on, "if Misty really is pregnant, which I doubt, it's not my baby. Okay, listen. This is Misty. When I told her I was going to school in California, did she say she would miss me? No. First she wanted to know if I could get her a paid-for trip by crying to my new 'rich' father that I couldn't live without her. Then, when I turned that down, she began to wonder if Mom wouldn't like to sort of 'adopt' her since she would be so lonely once we were gone." His grin was wide. "Hey, Misty is one sharp little operator. You can't trust a thing she says."

Shawnee made a face, exasperation chasing relief through her system. "But, Jimmy, why were you going out with a girl like that?"

He shrugged. "She's a fox, Mom. And she's funny when she's in the right mood. But I've never been serious about her. You know that."

No, she didn't know any such thing. But what the heck—she was just a mother, grimly hanging on for dear life. She wasn't expected to know things. Was she?

Turning to Ken, she looked into his laughing eyes, and suddenly she was laughing herself.

"You guys are going to get all mushy, I can tell," Jimmy said flippantly. "And I bet Lani needs some help with that ice. I'm out of here."

"Jimmy..." She caught hold of his hand and squeezed it. "I just want you to know how proud I am of you," she said softly, all her love in her eyes.

"Yeah, well..." He glanced away, embarrassed. "I love you, Mom," he muttered. Then slowly, very slowly, he turned and looked at Ken. "I—I love you, too, Dad," he said, his eyes huge and questioning, as though he wasn't sure how Ken would receive that news.

Ken tried to say something. He opened his mouth, but nothing came out. Blinded by sudden tears, he reached awkwardly for his son and took him in his arms, hugging him tight. "I love you, too, son," he whispered. "More than anything."

And it was almost true. He realized that as Jimmy drew away, laughing, blinking hard, grinning and turning to go. There had been a time when he had wondered if he would ever love Jimmy as much as Shawnee did. Now he knew. It was inevitable. His son was the most important thing in his life.

Except for one other.

Jimmy left, and Shawnee took his place in Ken's arms and they held each other tightly, laughing and crying at the same time.

"What a great kid he is," Ken kept repeating.

"The best," she agreed over and over again, looking up into his face, loving every line, every angle. "The best."

"Shawnee..." Drawing back, he looked down at her, his hands holding her face between them. "Shawnee, I'm not going to leave you here," he said fiercely. "Either you come with us or I'm going to put Jimmy in boarding school and come back here."

"What?" She was in shock. What did this mean? Ken's first priority had to be Jimmy. The whole point was for him to have time to get to know his son. "What are you talking about?"

"This." His kiss was hard and full, with a touch of masculine arrogance and more than a hint of desire. "I love you, Shawnee Caine," he said, his eyes still wet from the tears, his eyelashes clumped together as he glared down at her. "I have loved you since that first day I saw you working in the dusty country store. I loved you all that week as we got to know each other. I loved you all those years I thought I couldn't have you because you were already married. I loved you when I saw you again in that restaurant. And I love you now, more than ever. I won't leave you again. So you make the call. It's either here or there, but we're going to be together."

"Together?" Her voice warbled as though she couldn't quite get the concept.

"As in married," he told her firmly.

"Married?"

"Actually, what I'd like to do," he went on seriously, "is have you get someone to run your café for a year while you go to California with Jimmy and me. I'll spend most of the year wrapping up my law practice. Then, next summer, we'll all come back here for good. Would you like that?"

She sniffled and blinked at him, unable to respond as her eyes welled with tears.

He gazed at her, puzzled by her tears and lack of response. "Of course, if you don't like that, I could take Jimmy to school on the mainland and then come right back here. Or anything else you want." He pulled her close. "I just want to be with you, Shawnee. Whatever it takes. We've wasted too many years."

He stroked her hair for a moment as the sobbing grew more intense, then drew back and looked at her face.

"Shawnee?" he asked.

She couldn't speak. She was still crying. She knew her face was red and swollen, knew her makeup was all over the place and her eyes were going to be bloodshot. But she couldn't help it. She had to cry.

"Shawnee, honey, what's the matter?" He was beginning to get seriously worried. "Is something wrong? Did I say something?"

She shook her head vigorously, but still the tears came, still the sobs racked her body. Snuggling up against him, she buried her face against his chest and cried, a great upheaval of relief and the release of a tension that had gone on for much too long.

He patted her awkwardly and made soft, soothing noises. At last the storm began to pass. The sobs came fewer and further between, and the tears stopped flowing. He pulled away again, looking anxiously at her tear-stained face.

"What is it, darling? What can I do for you?"

"Nothing," she managed to whisper, and then she smiled and a sob made her hiccup. "Everything."

Suddenly it all seemed so simple. The pieces of the puzzle were sliding together as though there had never been a problem, even though just days before, the rough edges had kept them from seeming in any way compatible. What had held her back? What had made her doubt? There was no doubt any longer. She knew it was all true. It wasn't a fairy tale. Finally, she could believe.

"Ken," she got out jerkily. "I'm . . . so . . . happy."

And the tears began to flow again.

Ken pulled her back into his arms, but there was a frown on his face. "If this is happiness," he muttered, "I'd hate to see what you're going to do when you're sad."

"I'll never be sad again," she promised wetly, still sobbing. "Oh, Ken, I love you so much!"

"Prove it," he said, his voice low and husky, his kiss teasing her neck.

"Prove it?" Shock finally stopped the tears. She pulled back and stared at him, her cheeks wet. "Right now?"

His smile was slow and full of fire as he took in her lovely face, sealing it into his memory forever. "Right now."

She smiled back, touching his face with her hand. "You'd better lock the door," she whispered. "This may take a while."

"The rest of our lives," he murmured as he gathered her back into his arms and held her close. "The rest of our lives."

* * * * *

SPRING
fancy
'94

**They're sexy, single...
and about to get snagged!**

Passion is in full bloom as love catches
the fancy of three brash bachelors. You won't
want to miss these stories by three of
Silhouette's hottest authors:

CAIT LONDON
DIXIE BROWNING
PEPPER ADAMS

Spring fever is in the air this March—
and there's no avoiding it!

Only from  *Silhouette®*

where passion lives.

SF94

Coming in April from

SILHOUETTE®

Desire®

Jock's Boys

a new series by
Jennifer Greene

The sexy, single Connor brothers are each about to meet their perfect partners—with *lots* of help from a matchmaking pirate ghost named Jock.

BEWITCHED: April's *Man of the Month,* Zach, just wants to be left alone but finds it impossible with the arrival of one sexy single mother.

BOTHERED: In May, meet Seth, a man who gets a much-needed confidence boost with the woman of his dreams.

BEWILDERED: And in June, get to know Michael, a man who believes romance is for fools—till he meets his own true love.

"A spellbinding storyteller of uncommon brilliance, the fabulous JENNIFER GREENE is one of the romance genre's gifts to the world of popular fiction."

—Melinda Helfer, *Romantic Times*

SILHOUETTE® Desire®

JOAN JOHNSTON'S

HAWK'S WAY

SERIES CONTINUES!

Available in March, *The Cowboy Takes a Wife* (D #842) is the latest addition to Joan Johnston's sexy series about the lives and loves of the irresistible Whitelaw family. Set on a Wyoming ranch, this heart-wrenching story tells the tale of a single mother who desperately needs a husband—a very *big* husband—fast!

Don't miss *The Cowboy Takes a Wife* by Joan Johnston, only from Silhouette Desire.

SILHOUETTE Desire

COMING NEXT MONTH

#847 BEWITCHED—Jennifer Greene
Jock's Boys series

April's *Man of the Month*, Zach Connor, swore off family life long ago. But could he resist single mom Kirstin Grams and a matchmaking ghost who was intent on setting the two up?

#848 I'M GONNA GET YOU—Lass Small
Fabulous Brown Brothers

Tom Brown wanted Susan Lee McCrae, a honey-blond beauty with a streak of Texas stubbornness and a string of admirers. But he didn't want her just for now...he wanted her for always!

#849 MYSTERY LADY—Jackie Merritt
Saxon Brothers series

Sexy Rush Saxon was searching for riches, but found a floundering construction business and the last demure woman on earth. But Valentine LeClair held a secret she would never share with *this* ex-playboy.

#850 THE BRAINY BEAUTY—Suzanne Simms
Hazards, Inc. series

Egyptologist Samantha Wainwright had no time for an ex-Boy Scout doing a good deed. But for Jonathan Hazard, it wasn't just his job to protect this beauty...it was also his pleasure!

#851 RAFFERTY'S ANGEL—Caroline Cross

Years ago ex-agent Chase Rafferty had killed an innocent man. Now why was beautiful Maggie McKenna, the victim's wife, helping Chase get on with *his* life?

#852 STEALING SAVANNAH—Donna Carlisle

C.J. Cassidy needed to prove that he, was no longer a thief. But how could he when all he could think about was stealing Savannah Monterey's heart?

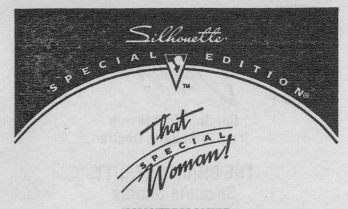

MYSTERY WIFE
Annette Broadrick

She awoke in a French hospital—and found
handsome Raoul DuBois, claiming she was his wife,
Sherye, mother of their two children. But she didn't
recognize him or remember her identity. Whoever she
was, Sherye grew more attached to the children every
day—and the growing passion between her and
Raoul was like nothing they'd ever known before....

She's friend, wife, mother—she's you! And beside
each Special Woman stands a wonderfully *special*
man. It's a celebration of our heroines—and the men
who become part of their lives.

Don't miss **THAT SPECIAL WOMAN!** each month—
from some of your special authors! Only from
Silhouette Special Edition!

TSW494